FELINE THE LOVE

RIVER'S EDGE SHIFTERS #2

LORELEI M. HART
ARIA GRACE

SURRENDERED PRESS

CONTENTS

ONE

LEO

I STRIPPED MY CLOTHES AND CALLED FORTH MY cat. I'd been in my skin for too many days and needed to stretch my legs and catch a mouse or two. It was less than ideal to leave my first-floor window open enough for me to climb through, but what else could I do? As crazy as the city was, people would notice if I went outside naked. No, that probably wasn't true, but they might notice the naked man turning into an animal.

Maybe.

Cities were weird like that.

And I actually thought city life might be for me.

I shimmied out the window and jumped down onto the concrete sidewalk. There were benefits to having an apartment in the back of the building, even if everyone, including the landlords, thought otherwise. They put all the fancy amenities, along with their higher rents, on the upper levels. And by fancy amenities, I meant a full-sized fridge.

This was most definitely not the life I anticipated while growing up in the fiercest lion pride in North America. Not once in all my pre-shift years did I suspect I was going to be any different than my fathers. Why would I? Not a single member of the pride ever had been, the whole recessive gene thing previously considered more of a fairy tale than science.

I even called my inner cat Lion. And he was strong— still was. He just didn't come with the huge body to go along with it.

When my first shift came and out popped my cat, the disappointment was clear on their faces. I was meant to be tough, strong, ferocious, and potentially the next alpha of the pride. Instead, I was a house cat. An everyday, run-of-the-mill kitty. And not even one of those huge cats that eat ex-husbands.

Which is why leaving the pride had been the right choice. My only choice, really. I'd been shunned from my first shift, and what kind of a life was that? *What kind of life was working from home and sneaking around to let your cat free?*

Moving to the city? That choice...not so right. But I was here, and I was making it work...ish.

My feet hit the pavement with a soft thud, and I scurried away from the window, avoiding the urine-soaked puddles as I went. My cat was on a mission. Operation: Hunt the Rat. At least the city was good for that. Rats were practically everywhere—everywhere except my building. We managed to deal with them my first year there.

Five years.

I'd been here five years. It was beginning to feel like it was time for a change.

Moving here, I expected a lot of different challenges from my life with the pride. I wouldn't have the structured safety nets, the comfort of being with other shifters, or the freedom to not have to hide who I was, and...maybe that was it. The longer I was away from them, the less I remembered why it was so hard to leave in the first place.

Once I got here, I realized those differences weren't so internal. There were more physical dangers for me to worry about, like cars to dodge and recognizing the people who were animals but not all in the shifter way. I knew I'd have to hide who I was, of course. But what I hadn't expected was that my biggest danger wouldn't come from those hardened by city life or the vehicles they drove. Nope. They would come in the form of little old ladies who thought they had to save the world.

By saving the world, I mean they liked to trap the "adorable stray kitties" and bring them to the shelter. I had more than one close call, including escaping in the shelter's parking lot as some blue-hair tried to get me out of her car. I still got chills just thinking about it, knowing full well the first course of action was always a neuter.

Now I sort of knew the areas to avoid people who were helpful, but it took some trial and error. Spoiler alert, adult clubs are just as likely to try to rescue a stray animal as little old ladies with nothing to do. So, when I needed to hunt, I stuck to hanging out behind galleries, businesses that were closed permanently, and some of the seedier neighborhoods people avoided after dark. It wasn't ideal, but it worked for me.

Of course, the occasional homeless person would want to say hello. I usually let them pet me, as demeaning as most of my pride probably would've thought it was. Their lives were hard enough without being rejected by a cat. If I could give them even a tiny bit of happiness, there was no reason not to.

I turned down my new favorite alley. They had done some renovating of one of the buildings and all the rats scurried to find new homes, making it ideal hunting territory. City hunting required different skills than hunting in the wild. Here, I looked for things humans left behind, such as their garbage. In the wild, I looked for footprints and grasses that had been brushed aside.

It kept my cat on his toes, which was good since he was cooped up far too often.

Out of the corner of my eye, I caught movement behind the dumpster and got ready to pounce. It was a larger shadow than I usually saw in this part of the city, and I wanted to make sure it wasn't a skunk. No one needs that, and for some reason, they had been more prevalent the past couple of months.

Behind me, a door opened, but I ignored it. Chances were it was someone going out for the night, and they wouldn't even see me.

"Here, kitty, kitty, kitty, kitty, kitty. Here, kitty, kitty, kitty, kitty."

Fuck, I was wrong. They were out there for me.

I snapped around to take in the full picture and saw a woman standing there with a dish of what smelled like tuna in her hand. But she wasn't the one who worried me. It was the man next to her with a laundry basket behind his back.

"Here, sweet girl," she called. "You're a pretty girl, aren't you?" She ducked down and set the dish on the floor as the man stepped closer to her side.

"You really need to have a Mom and Papa take care of you. We can't have you roaming around all those cars. And there are some bad people," she whispered, talking to me like I could understand. Granted, I could understand her, but she had no way of knowing that. Heck, she thought I was a girl because...I'm a cat. "Let us help you find a new home."

I looked back to the dumpster to see if there was a way out behind it instead of running past the man who was getting ready to lunge at me with his makeshift cage. The gate was closed but not bolted. I decided to chance it, taking off as fast as my feet could carry me. The woman continued to call me while the man told her he was right and the plan was doomed from the beginning.

I snuck through the fencing and opted to go straight home. Fuck the hunting. Fuck the city. Fuck the people who thought they were helping.

It was official. I was done with city life. How I managed this long was a freaking miracle. I was just too damn tired. Tired of not being able to run free. Tired of hiding who I was even in my own home, needing my shades drawn and a fake litter box just in case someone stopped by, which they never did but with landlords you never knew. Sure, there were nights I chose to sleep in a ball on my own pillow instead of as a man, but that just wasn't the kind of life I longed for.

I climbed back in my window, shifted in my bedroom in case someone was looking, then locked the window tight and pulled the shades. After a quick shower to get the scent of the city off me, I climbed into bed with my laptop. I'd been thinking about moving for a while but the fear of big changes kept getting in my way. But tonight kinda sealed the deal.

I needed to get out of here.

I pulled up a real estate site on my laptop and put in the criteria for the kind of place I was looking for: Riverfront property with lots of acreage. That was pretty much it. I didn't even choose a location. I had nothing tying me to any particular town.

Over three thousand properties met my criteria, and I filtered the results by price—lowest to highest. I was doing well financially, saving a lot of money each month thanks to my low-rent apartment and lack of social life. And I also had the money my parents gave me when I left the pride—not out of desire to do so, but out of tradition. Of course, it was meant to be a gift to a lion's new pride when he mated. Unfortunately, I met none of those criteria, but it was still nice to have a safety net in case I needed it. It was even nicer that I hadn't needed to touch one penny so far, and I wasn't about to change that by purchasing a property out of my price range.

I needed something that would give my cat freedom to roam, not anything fancy or pretentious.

The first few places that popped up were mislabeled and were actually rental properties. They were cute enough, but if they were renting for prices that got confused with sales prices, then they really weren't what I needed or could afford. Besides that, rentals came with landlords taking away some of the freedom I'd been hoping to find.

I scrolled past those and the listings that were basically land with a hunting shack they were calling a house. One such shack was only two hundred square feet and had no windows. It wasn't even functional enough to qualify as one of those fancy new tiny homes.

Then there were four that had clauses saying the buyer would need to sign a waiver due to possible contaminants. I was a hard pass on those.

But then I saw one with a gorgeous river out back, outside of the house's view.

As is—has potential.

The words should've sent me scrolling. Who wants potential when they could have move-in-ready splendor? Me, apparently, because I couldn't move past the listing. It had the acreage I wanted, the home was unseen by the road, and the price was low enough that fixing the *as is* parts couldn't be that bad...probably.

I clicked on the pictures over and over again. It didn't go unnoticed that most of them were of the outdoors and not of the house. The house was either dated or needed major attention. But I could work with that. Asbestos mold waivers...not so much, but wiring and sheet rock...I could handle. I'd probably even enjoy it.

It was close enough to the city that if I *had* to drive in for a work meeting, I could. But since I was telecommuting 99% of the time anyway, I didn't see that as being a huge issue.

I filled out the interest form, and was surprised to get an immediate response back. But then again, real estate was a *eat-what-you-kill* career, so people had to act fast. As a cat myself, I kind of respected that.

The email stated the house was currently being looked at, and if I wanted to make an appointment to see it, I should do so sooner rather than later.

I doubted that was true. It sounded more like a sales technique than reality...but what if it was true...

So, I did what any rational person would do.

I submitted a full-price offer.

"What brings you here today?" Jase came out onto the porch with sweet Angeline, who was fidgeting to get down, in his arms. She wasn't in his arms for long, though. Now that she found her legs, she was bound and determined to use them even if she fell more often than not.

"I just thought I'd stop by and say hi to Lux." Lux bolted off the porch and straight to me at the sound of his name. I had an affinity for that cat, three-legged and all. He'd just wormed his way into my heart. "You remind me of Grandma Angeline." I scooped him into my arms. August's grandma held a kindness I'd never seen in another person. I missed her, and my visits to Lux were more about that than anything else.

August and Jase were doing an amazing job keeping her legacy alive, and little Angeline lit up the room with her grandmother's smile.

Lux jumped from my arms as baby Angeline decided to make her way over to me on her toddling legs. "When did you become such a big girl?"

She giggled and it was a beautiful sound. She stopped in front of me with her arms up, so I picked her up, settling her on my shoulders.

At one point, I had thought I would get married, have 3.5 kids, and live the good life. That didn't quite work out.

My life was hardly what you called awful, but the getting married thing just hadn't happened. Small towns had small populations. It was basic math. And sadly, in this small population, the right person, the one I'd hoped to share my life with, just wasn't here. And yes, I believed in one true love and all that, which didn't help matters.

But why settle down with an omega you didn't adore?

If I wanted my dream life, I had to give up my home, my job, and my friends to try to find someone in another town. But I wasn't willing to give up all the good I had now for a someday-maybe. I just needed to accept the fact that it was okay to be alone. I was almost there.

Most days it didn't bother me.

Some days, like today, it seemed like a little splinter that you couldn't find, and didn't really bother you, except for when it suddenly annoyed you a little bit. That's what it was like today.

"You sure you don't want some tea?" August came out and joined his husband with a box of tea in his hand.

"Well, if the water's already hot." They were such good friends. They never questioned my weirdness about visiting the cat or even the one time they caught me talking to Daisy like she was a person and not a pig —who thought she was a dog.

We went inside and sat down with Angeline in her highchair. I opened the cookie tin on the center of the table. It always had homemade cookies inside. It was nice to see that August kept up that tradition.

I handed one to Angeline, and her face lit up with the joy of the oatmeal goodness. I didn't blame her. Their cookies never failed to be made of yumminess.

"Anything new and exciting in the world of real estate?" I asked as August slid me a mug of tea.

"Okay," he said noncommittally. He'd recently started to work at the local agency doing property listings and some internet sales. It was a new technology for the area, and while it had some benefits, most of the people who wanted homes here were not that tech savvy. At least not from what I'd seen. "Not too much." But I felt like there was something more that he wasn't saying.

His husband sat next to him, pride for his mate beaming out.

"Well, just that..." Jase nudged.

"A couple sales." August grabbed a cookie. "I sold Xander's old place." He was careful not to refer to it as Clarence's. I didn't blame him. Clarence had been pure evil filled with alcohol, and things almost ended really badly for August because of it. Technically, it was Clarence's, though, which sucked. It would've been nice for Xander to at least get a college fund out of the sale.

No one missed Clarence after he drank a bottle of bourbon and ended up face down in the river. I don't even think Xander missed him. He might've been the man he knew as his dad for most of his life, but he was an abusive asshole.

"Well, that's good," I said. "It's gonna need a lot of work. Hope they know that going in." It was a miracle the building was still standing.

"I tried to tell him." August picked up a cookie piece Angeline had dropped. "He just put in a full-price offer, sight unseen."

"The bank was happy to get it." Jase was so proud of his husband. It was adorable.

And he was right. Around here, foreclosures tended not to sell for years, and when they did, it was generally a neighbor who couldn't stand to see it empty and attracting wild critters.

"I thought you had some big company nibbling at that place." At least that had been the rumor around town.

But then again, there was a rumor around town that the library was being painted green and it spread to the point of someone calling a town meeting with signatures protesting the nonexistent plan. The joy of small towns.

"I did." August smirked. "It's amazing how many things you can find wrong with a place when you really put your mind to it. And then, you know, hearing the stories about how our zoning board hadn't approved anything in over a year didn't help."

Technically, the zoning board hadn't had anything to vote on in at least a year.

"My husband is saying he made sure they didn't want it."

"Good." The idea of a factory coming to town had made me nervous. It made a lot of people nervous.

"We don't need to be building up here." August held the cookie tin out for me. "I know factories need to be made, but our town can't support one."

He wasn't wrong. As a small community, we were getting along just fine. We weren't one of those towns where unemployment was high and education was low after the boom left. We didn't need a factory to come in and save us, while actually destroying us in the process.

In fact, we didn't have the workers to support a factory even if one was built. Our small town would need to grow with lower-end jobs based on the company's specs. Nope, I wasn't sad to see someone snagged the place instead.

"I'm glad you found a new owner." I grabbed one more cookie then stood up. "I best get going. I don't need to be pissing off the boss man."

Sheriff Martin was a bonafide asshat who liked to use his power for his own entertainment. How he ever got voted into that position in the first place was beyond me. Now it was a forgone conclusion that he'd always win. But at one point, he ran against someone else and won. That blew my mind.

"Thanks for the tea." I made a silly face at Angeline, and she repaid me with her giggles. "I needed it."

"I miss her too." August looked up at me in understanding.

I got back into town later than I wanted and walked in to find Sheriff Martin talking with the new office clerk,

Ms. Patty. And by talking, I mean a pathetic attempt at flirting. She was having no part of that. And he should've known better. Ms. Patty was happily married to her childhood sweetheart.

But the flirting wasn't new. He did it the day she came in for an interview, yet somehow she still thought it was a good idea to work here.

I gave her a week before she decided to take one of the positions open at the town hall or the public library. The extra dollar per hour she was getting here was so not worth this.

"How are things going?" I interrupted their little chat.

"It's quiet on this front," Sheriff Martin said, stepping back. He hadn't been close enough to be *too close* or inappropriate in a way I could call him on, but it felt off. Then again, lots of things felt off when it came to him.

"Good." I gave Ms. Patty a wave. "I like quiet."

"Yeah, well, I heard Clarence's place sold, so we're gonna have to keep an eye on that and make sure there's no riff raff moving in." And by we, he meant me. "We don't need riff raff coming into town and bringing us down."

Riff raff. As if Clarence were the epitome of town glory. He was an abusive piece-of-shit drunk. The only reason people put up with him as long as they did was because they loved his wife.

He loved her too, but when cancer stole her, he crumbled even further into horribleness.

Finding out she had been unfaithful over a decade earlier had been his undoing. He should've been thrown in jail for the crap he pulled at Angeline's old place, but I wasn't in charge. And really, having Xander safe had been enough at the time.

"I'm sure they'll be fine." And more than sure they would be better than Clarence.

"Heard he got a full-price offer," Ms. Patty added. She would know. She loved the town rumor mill. Thinking about it, that was probably why she took this job.

"Oh, so he's one of those rich city folks." Sheriff Martin sneared.

"I didn't say that." Patty gave him *the eye,* the one that dared him to put words in her mouth. Maybe I was worrying about her for nothing. I hoped so.

"Keep an eye on it, Ron. We gotta make sure this town keeps itself up." He marched off.

Asshat.

"How are things going, Ms. Patty?"

Ms. Patty had taught preschool years ago, and somehow, her teacher name stuck. "Good. I'm learning so much about law enforcement." She smiled brightly.

"Let me know if there's anything I can help you with." She would probably tell Sheriff Martin to kiss her ass by week's end, but for now, the position was filled and she was holding her own.

"Will do. I'm gonna go work on fixing up the mess you two call filing." Yeah, it was pretty bad. Sheriff Martin and I didn't know anything about organizing or filing systems. "So, let me know if we get a call."

"Will do." I took a seat at my desk and went over the logs from my off time.

"Remember what I said about Clarence's old place," Sheriff Martin barked as he walked past my desk and toward the door.

"I won't forget to check him out...after he moves in." What did he think I should do? Preemptively find the guy? "I'll make sure he's not riff raff." Better me than the sheriff checking out the new owners. My boss didn't make a good first impression. Or a second or third, either.

THREE

LEO

I TURNED MY U-HAUL TRUCK DOWN THE LONG dirt drive that led to my new house. A house. I wasn't sure which surprised me more—that I was a home-owner in the middle of nowhere or that I purchased said home sight unseen. Closing the deal via the internet had been much easier than I thought it'd be.

I'd left the city expecting to be second-guessing myself for a while, but as I drove from city to suburb to the middle of nowhere, I found peace. This was where I was meant to be. The land was gorgeous. No, it was beyond gorgeous. The trees..the birds...the lack of traffic...just perfect.

And then it got less perfect.

I started to see a tire here, some empty bottles there... Then the junk started piling up and then more junk. Nothing too terrible, but not a good omen for what was ahead. Around the bend, I avoided holes in the hard-pack as the house came into view. The house, or rather the dilapidated shack, that was now my new home.

I pulled to a stop and climbed out of the car, taking a deep breath.

The scent of moss tickled my nose. It had always been a favorite of mine. And in the far-off distance, I could hear the sound of the river.

The building was just a building—it could be fixed. But the scent and sounds of nature surrounding me, that was either there or it wasn't. And this place had it. My home had it. Inside, my cat purred. He was going to have a grand time exploring this place. For a moment, I was completely happy and content.

And then the staleness of the house hit me.

I walked toward the house, and the closer I got, the worse it smelled and the more cracks and chipped paint came into sight. The first step onto the porch creaked, the second step wobbled, the third step started to sink from the years of neglect and decay.

As is, has potential.

They hadn't been wrong. But I could do this. I could find the potential and make this house a home.

The door was already unlocked, if the lock even worked, so I pushed it open. The stench filling my senses was like steel alcohol, cigarettes, and...yeah...a dead animal or two.

At least I hoped it was an animal.

As is, has potential. I can do this.

I stepped inside, and the room was completely full. No one had bothered to move a single thing. From the ashtray on the table to the empty beer bottles on the floor to the three-quarters-empty bottle of gin sitting next to the recliner... It was like the previous owner went out for the mail and never came back. I felt like I had walked into an episode of one of those hoarding shows, only this one was a time capsule of hoarding grossness.

I walked through each room, opening all the windows. If I was going to work in there without puking, I needed to get the stench out.

I also needed a dumpster, possibly two. Not only would I have all the trash to remove, but also the construction debris.

There was a shit ton of things to do after the mess was hauled away. New windows, a new roof, new flooring, and new walls. The place needed just about everything. But it was all doable, and all stuff I had the skill set to handle. Growing up in the pride, I learned a great deal of hands-on skills. I could work on an engine, build a house from the ground up, and mend a quilt. It was the way of the lion to work together while still being self-sufficient.

At least until a domestic house cat came into the picture. We were a team for others. If someone's car broke down, people all pitched in to help. If their roof sprung a leak, it was the same. But when it came to me and my truck losing its power steering, the help was not exactly forthcoming.

I shook that memory away and started to make a mental list of all the things I needed. I just hoped the lumber yards delivered this far out.

When I finally made it back outside, I was grateful for the fresh air to clear my lungs. That was when a couple of outbuildings caught my eye. They hadn't been on the listing, and by the looks of them, they weren't up to code so I could understand why. The first one was filled with junk, and not the good kind with some hidden antique treasures that could make me a few bucks. Unfortunately, it was mostly bags of trash, boxes of broken windows and doors from who knew when, and a junk car.

The second was mostly empty, which was good because I needed a place to put all my furniture. It sure as shit wasn't going in the house until I got it cleaned up.

I drove up to the building and spent the rest of the afternoon unpacking the trailer. There really wasn't much in it, thankfully. I still had to return the trailer to the closest city, as they called it. It was more like a town, but much larger than where I would be calling home.

"I look like a college kid." I laughed at myself because it was true.

After everything was unpacked, I drove back down the dirt driveway and returned my trailer. The drive there wasn't too bad. Short enough that if I wanted to go to bigger stores, it wouldn't be a big deal, but far enough away that I'd at least think twice about it.

I missed my turn and ended up in a little cul-de-sac neighborhood and went to turn around in a driveway. I didn't know if it was fate or what, but sitting in that driveway was a *For Sale by Owner* sign on a camper, and a lightbulb in my head went off. I could buy a camper and use it for my home while I fixed up the main house. Afterward, I could sell it or keep it—whatever. It was better than sleeping in that stench or driving to a hotel each day. That was for sure.

I knocked on the door and out came the owner who was more than happy to show me his pride and joy. The pride and joy his new wife told him he needed to get rid of.

She wasn't going to "pay his debts," as he explained it. We worked out a quick deal then drove to the nearest bank. As soon as he had the cash in his hands, I drove off with my new camper in tow.

I ended the long day by cleaning out the dusty trailer enough to get some sleep. Tomorrow, I'd order a dumpster and begin creating my new life.

It was gonna be a good one. I could feel it. As awful as that house was, I felt like I was home for the first time in a very long time.

FOUR
RON

"Did you take care of that?" Sheriff Martin stood over me as I was typing up a report for the town council. I had no idea what he was talking about. "It's been a week since the papers were signed."

Oh, right. He wanted me to pester the new guy in town for no other reason than we could.

"I have it on my list for today." Now I did, anyway. It was better for me to go out there and introduce our new resident to the local law enforcement. At least I would be cordial, unlike the sheriff, unless he took a shine to the owner. Honestly, I was surprised he wanted me to go instead of him. The one thing the man did love above all else was meeting new people he could intimidate by throwing around his power.

"I'll go as soon as I finish typing this up," I promised.

"Ms. Patty can do it." And she could. It was just copying the financial data that was easy enough for her to take care of.

"I sure can." She jumped up and waved me away. "Go pester those poor new owners for us." She smirked. Somehow the sheriff didn't notice her sarcasm. "It must be hard moving here from the city."

She was right. It had to be. We had none of the amenities they'd be used to. I wasn't even sure if they could get a decent satelite out there for the internet with all the trees and hills. And there was no fancy takeaway here. We didn't even have a Chinese restaurant.

He was in for a rude awakening before he saw how bad the house was. That blasted thing needed to be razed. It was a shack long before it was vacant, and being vacant never did anything to improve a place.

I left the office, stopping at the diner for a quick sandwich before driving up to Clarence's old place. Not once had I been up there for something good. At least this time wouldn't involve suspected violence. Although, the new guy was probably seeing red over having bought the house in the first place.

As I pulled up in front of the house, I wasn't surprised when a dumpster came into view.

The bank had decided it would be cheaper in the long run to just sell it exactly as it was— complete with all the crap inside. And I could see their point. They could fix it up and sell it, but in this location, they'd spend more time and money on it than they'd get in return.

What did surprise me as I pulled to a stop was the camper trailer set in between the house and the outbuildings. Whoever bought the house was clever. It had to be easier to live in a trailer than the house.

I put the car in park and climbed out. A motion on the porch caught my eye. Not a person. It was a cat. And not just any cat, the most beautiful cat I'd ever seen. Its calico fur paired perfectly with its bright green eyes.

Not that I'd ever admit to Lux that I found a more beautiful cat. Lux would hold it against me forever. Cats were like that. They were strong-willed, independent, and didn't care about impressing you. It was what made them awesome.

Dogs were fine and all, but I was definitely a cat man.

As if it could tell, the cat pranced over to me.

"You're a sweet baby," I called out, and the prancing became more of a run. I squatted and held my hand out.

His fur was shiny with no mats. He wasn't exactly what I'd call plump, but he was definitely well-fed.

He rubbed his chin against me, and I picked him up. The only thing I didn't like about my place was the inability to have a cat.

"Aren't you a good boy."

He rolled in my arm for me to pet his belly, and that was when I noticed that he was in fact a boy, and he was intact.

Why did people do that? "Looks like I need to have a talk with your owner." We had enough feral cats in these woods without adding more to the population. "I think he forgot to have you snipped."

The cat froze in my arms as if he knew what I was saying, and he jumped down.

"Is your papa home?" I asked, not expecting the cat to do anything, but hoping the owner might hear me and come on out.

The cat looked up at me, did a weird bob thing with his head, and then shot off towards the house.

"I'll take that as a yes." I brushed off the fur from my uniform and closed the distance between me and the house, climbing up to the steps while being sure to skip the one I knew was about to cave.

I'd been at this place too many times over the years and knew which steps, floorboards, and chairs to avoid.

At first, I was sad Xander didn't get the place. It had been his home for much of his life, but then I saw him after only being with Doc a few months. He was so filled with joy, and all the fear that had always been just below the surface was finally gone. He was better off without this place...and those memories.

I hated that I couldn't have done anything sooner, but I just didn't have enough ammunition to get Xander into a better place without making his life worse.

He was happy now. I just had to keep reminding myself that. "Hello," I called into the open door. "Anybody home?"

"Just a second." A man came into view wearing only his jeans with a shirt in his hands.

My eyes were drawn to his bare chest, every single muscle of it defined so clearly. I wanted to run my fingers across each plane. No, that was a lie. I wanted to trace a path with my tongue.

I closed my eyes and shook my head once, trying to get the sudden burst of lust cleared from it as I ignored the tightening of my uniform slacks. *Do not look at his chest.*

I shouldn't have to remind myself to be professional, but I did. There was just something about this man, and if I didn't get myself under control soon, he was going to think I was a perv. What was wrong with me?

When I opened my eyes again, he was pulling the hem of his shirt down.

"Sorry about that." He didn't hide the smirk on his face. At least he wasn't offended by my bout of unprofessionalism. "What can I do for you, Officer?"

"You can call me Ron." For some reason, I didn't want him to be formal with me. "I was just being neighbor-ly." I smiled and cleared my throat. "Neighborly and nosy, I guess. My friend August said he sold this place, so I wanted to stop by and give you a proper River's Edge welcome."

He held out his hand to shake mine. "I'm Leo. I guess there's no hiding in small towns, is there?"

"I suppose there's not." No supposing to it. There wasn't.

"Not that I have anything to hide," he quickly added on.

"Yeah, I wasn't worried about that." Certainly not as much as I was worried about him noticing my attrac-tion to him. Which was insane. I'd never been drawn to a stranger like this. Sure, I saw guys and thought they looked yum. But this? This was different, and I wasn't sure how I felt about it. "How're things going in the house? It was kind of left a shithole." A complete shithole.

"It's...going." He shrugged. "I'm just mostly spending my time hauling stuff out of here." He signalled for me to step inside. The living room was almost empty, so I could tell he'd been working hard.

"After that's done, I'll start demolition and throw even more stuff in the dumpster. My guess is as big as that dumpster is, it's gonna need to be emptied again." Again? How much shit did Clarence have packed in here?

"The camper working out for you?" I asked cautiously. The idea was genius, but I didn't see any power hook-ups, and an irrational need to protect him had me oddly worried about his well-being.

"Yeah, I figured that was easier than trying to get any of this disaster clean enough to use or driving to a hotel since there's not really a hotel in town."

"We've got a few rooms to rent, but yeah, no real hotel. I guess it's not the same, and with your pet cat, your options are a bit limited."

"He'd be fine here for the night, but no, it's not the same as a hotel. But that's okay. I knew when I left the city that this place would take some adjusting to."

"Disappointed in the house?" Because I sure as hell would be.

"The house...could be better. I really do love this property, though. It just feels like home."

I wasn't sure what home felt like, and seeing the glimmer of happiness in his eyes as he said it, I wanted to so badly. I liked my place well enough, and this town was where I belonged, but home was something entirely different.

"Here's my card." I handed him a card from my front pocket. "I'm off tomorrow if you want some help around here. Four hands are better than two." Lame. I was officially lame.

He cocked his head as if he was looking at me from under the brim of a cowboy hat. "Is that what sheriffs do in these here parts?"

I smiled at the cheesy accent he added to his question. He was clearly teasing me. "I'm the deputy, but no, this isn't part of my job description. I just like to help people." But mostly just him because I wanted to eat him up. I mean, I liked helping people in general because it made me feel productive, like I was contributing. I'd been that way for as long as I could remember. "I could help you throw the rest of this shit out. I don't know much about construction, but I can throw out trash like a boss."

"You know what, I think I'd like that."

I knew I would. "I'll see you tomorrow then."

"I can't wait."

FIVE
LEO

WHAT HAD I BEEN THINKING WHEN I SAID HE could come over?

I'd already gotten most of the junk out of the main living area, and when the officer came by, I was taking a break. A cat break.

It felt so good to be able to shift at will. My cat was loving it. More than once, I let him out to chase off the plethora of things crawling in the dilapidation that was my home. That wasn't what he liked best. My cat loved to sit in the grass, soaking in the sun. Back in the city, outside time had been reserved for the night when it was easier to hide. But here, time and daylight didn't play a part in our decision making process.

Although, the distant sounds of wild animals might keep him close at night. My dads would have found that funny—or not, I didn't even know. They'd all but excommunicated me. But to them, our family were the wild animals to be feared in the night.

Of course, they had been spouting that when they thought I would grow up to be a mighty beast and not a pussy cat—literally.

Had I been anybody but their omega son, they'd have excommunicated me. Of that I was sure. But as the Pride Alpha, my dad played the part of loving father, saying we could make it work while treating me like something stinky on the bottom of his shoe. He didn't even let me participate in pride activities. In so many ways, it was worse than being kicked out.

They said we could make it work in public, but in private, that *work* had a very different meaning. They put up with me because they had to, and in their own way, they loved me. I think. But I crushed every expectation they had of what our family would look like long-term, and there was no way around that.

But it wasn't like I had a say in my recessive gene pool. That was all on them.

I allowed the pretense that the door was at least partially open for me to come back when I left the pride. It was better for my father, and part of me was scared to leave the only life I'd ever known. Having the possibility of returning if I needed to gave me the strength to move on.

And move on I did. Not that I had a lot to show for it just yet.

I was tempted to call Ron and tell him I didn't need his help after all. It really wasn't the best idea to be alone with the man. My cat, the one that was so quick to obey me and give me the reins, was in full-force, power positioning when the man was around. He'd even pushed me back enough to get cuddles from the guy. The only reason I regained control was because Ron mentioned cutting off our balls.

Although, my cat chanting *mate, mate, mate* through my mind as I chatted with the guy didn't help much either. But he was definitely wrong about that. Ron couldn't be my mate. He was human.

And as nice as he seemed, human and mate didn't exactly go together. It was just a fact. Never in the entire history of our pride, had a lion successfully taken a human mate. And the one failed attempt I was aware of hadn't been a simple *this isn't working out* thing. Unfortunately, blood was shed...in abundance.

My cat was just taking our instant attraction to officer hottie, paired with our need to get laid, as more than it was.

I still couldn't believe my cat had to go up to him and rub against him. Then he rolled on his back in such an obvious plea. *Give me attention! Give me attention!* How freaking embarrassing. I wasn't even in heat. Only true cats did that. I wish I had that as an excuse, but it was just my cat being all possessive and desperate.

And then Ron turned out to be so nice and funny and obviously interested. In the city, cops didn't just show up at your place for no reason. In the country, it seemed like they sort of did, and not only when they were on duty. Today was his day off, and Ron was on his way over to help me empty the house full of grossness. Of course, there was the possibility that he was coming out of curiosity more than anything else. But, still, he was coming.

And there was no hiding the disaster that was the house. At least he knew it wasn't me who was the pig. *This isn't a date.* Except it felt like one.

This was a very bad idea.

I climbed out of the trailer with my phone in hand, ready to walk over to the one area on the land that had reception. Before I could dial, he pulled in with his pickup truck and climbed out, giving me a little wave. Too late to cancel now.

He looked so different wearing civilian clothes. Although, all I could really see was a nice tight-fitting gray shirt. He looked amazing. How was it even possible for him to look better than in his uniform?

Mate.

Damn, my cat needed to simmer down. Thinking like that was only going to get us in a pickle.

"Hi," I called as he opened the truck door and climbed out.

"Good to see ya." He walked around the truck and grabbed a toolbox. "I'm not really good at fixing up stuff, but I've got some tools that might come in handy if we need to break things up to help them fit in the dumpster."

That was a mighty big tool box for someone who didn't use tools, and I was grateful for its presence. I only had the bare minimum as far as tools went. My savings was going to weep when I eventually hit the homestore.

I laughed as I thought about a show I watched just before my move. "You ever see those home shows where couples just take sledgehammers to kitchens and they act like they demolished things all day long when all they did was break one thing and then the construction crew came in and did it right?" Everyone had to break at least one wall or countertop under the guise of adding sweat equity.

He nodded and shifted the box from one hand to the other. "It is fun, I'd imagine. Breaking the cabinets you've always hated."

He had a point.

"It's safe to say there will be plenty to break today. Nothing in that house, including the walls, are worth saving." I showed him inside, surprised he knew which step to avoid completely.

"Yesterday, I finished emptying most of the house." I had so much energy and needed to wear my cat out. The way he was pouncing within me, he was going to shift in the middle of the night while I was asleep, just so he could get to Ron.

Mate.

He really needed to cut that shit out.

"I got the main bedroom, the living room, and the kitchen completely emptied. I still need to get things like the carpets and appliances out, but the big stuff is all gone." I walked down the short hallway and stopped in one of the two rooms left to conquer. "There are another two bedrooms to finish. That's pretty much it before I go to town on the carpets and such."

I was officially going to look into permits to add on a second story or possibly lengthen the home. It was much smaller than the dimensions made it look, and I couldn't quite figure out how that was the case. But it was. And adding on was easier than taking things down to the beams and beginning again, especially since I had to do that with the rest of the place.

"How are you doing this?" He set his tool box down and looked at me.

"I just bring them out to the porch and make sure there's nothing worth saving." I laughed and looked around the room. "So far, nothing has been worth saving."

"And outside because of the rodents?" He pointed to a pile of evidence of said rodents.

"Pretty much, yeah." I chuckled.

We carried the boxes out and looked through them. Most of them were women's clothing, some romance novels, and a few random knick knacks like gnomes and elves. I put a few aside to give to the local charity shop if Jase and August didn't think Xander would want them. They could be cleaned up well enough.

The clothes were a different matter altogether. The moisture had created black mold and I doubted it had any hopes of being cleaned enough to be reused, which was a shame. At one time, these had been someone's wardrobe, and now...not even good enough to be rags.

"It's weird seeing all her stuff," Ron said after about the fifth box.

"August mentioned that Xander's mother died years ago." He and his family had come over on my second night to make sure everything was alright and to bring me some food, which I appreciated.

At first, I thought it was just a realtor welcome wagon thing since we did everything online, but I soon realized it was more than that. And as they shared their mating story, I got it. I got why this house mattered. The story of Xander and his father broke my heart. No boy should be put through that.

"I'm assuming this was all hers."

Ron hummed in agreement as he tossed some nail polish bottles into a bag. "And you're looking through it in hopes of finding something for him?"

I shrugged.

We kept going through things, the stench and heaviness of the task the only thing keeping my erection at bay. Why did Ron have to smell so good, all orange blossom and honey? He was pretty much sunshine.

With each subsequent box, it became obvious we weren't going to salvage much of anything, which was a shame. It would've been nice to have kept some things for the boy.

I didn't lose my parents in the way he did, but in a way, I did lose them. And it sucked. The few things I had that reminded me of them meant something. I couldn't imagine if I lost them completely and had nothing of theirs to look at—to hold. And his loss was total. In theory, I could go back home and build something with my parents. He'd never see his mother again.

The next room didn't look like it had too much.

"This room is...it's like he just left." I snapped my mouth shut when I remembered what had happened...and why the boy had to suddenly leave his home or risk more abuse by his father.

"Yeah, that was Xander's room. Doc didn't want to get anything more than he could carry the first night. Clarence was...problematic."

I didn't look as hard to find things to save from this room. Any clothing would be outgrown, and that was pretty much all there was aside from a mattress and nightstand.

"Everyone in town seems nice," I said as I was deciding on whether or not to keep a photograph of what looked like a townwide festival. It was moldy and water-stained and ended up in the dumpster, but it stirred something in me. From the looks of things, the entire town had gathered to celebrate something. It reminded me of my pride. Given I already met a rabbit here, it wasn't too far-fetched that there were more shifters. But even if most of the people in the photo were, it wouldn't be the same as my pride.

But maybe that was better.

"Yeah, it's a pretty good town. Got a few bad seeds because, well, everywhere does, but for the most part, you'll like it here." Ron's stomach growled. "Been to the diner yet? They make the best pancakes."

I raised an eyebrow. "Do they use real syrup or pancake syrup?"

"Oooh, my man knows his pancakes."

His. Did he mean it? No, I wasn't going to let my mind wander down that path. He was nice, attractive, and we got along well. That was it. I merely grinned. "Well?"

"They have both because some people, for some reason I will never understand, still prefer the cheap stuff."

I grimaced. "I guess it's fine if you don't know what real maple syrup tastes like, but if it is, there's no comparison."

"Exactly. So, after we clean out the last of this room. Maybe we can go grab some?" Was he suggesting a date? Was the sexy alpha in uniform asking me on a date?

"Yeah, I'd like that." *Mine.* "My camper's great and all, but I've been eating instant food that you can make with a hot pot, and I'm kind of ready for some real food." Even the food my new friends brought over had been just okay, thanks to being unable to heat it up.

"Sounds like a plan." Plan. He said it's a plan, not a date. Not that I should date a human. Nope. That wasn't going to happen. Especially not a human my cat was in a frenzy over.

We emptied the last of his room and started to walk out when Ron froze, staring at the paneled wall. "You know what?" He looked at one end of the house then to the other. "It feels like there's more to this place than we're seeing."

"I know what you mean. I was thinking that earlier today. I just can't pinpoint exactly what it is that's off. It's like the bedrooms are too small."

"Mind if I use my hammer?" he asked.

"Go for it." Not that I had any clue what I was giving him permission to do, but given that nothing in the place was salvageable, what damage could he really manage?

"I'm wondering..." He went over to the wall he'd been eyeing, then went back to his tool box and grabbed both the hammer and a crowbar. "Let's pull this siding off just for shits and giggles."

"It has to come down anyway." The thing was warped and mushy.

The two of us ripped the first, then the second panel down, and instead of finding insulation and another half to the wall, we found ourselves looking into another room. A room that was hidden between the two bedrooms. It wasn't large, but it was full.

"So, this is a surprise." I blinked, almost wondering if it were real.

He just shook his head. "Yeah, it definitely is."

"Instant noodles and a secret room?" There was no way I wanted to leave this until later.

"Instant noodles and a secret room!"

We both spoke at the same time as we stared into our discovery.

SIX

RON

WHEN I WENT OVER TO THE OLD CLARENCE place, I expected hard work, possibly a little bit of flirting with the intriguing omega, and maybe a new friendship. I hadn't expected to find a hidden room, especially not one that looked like it jumped off the screen of a horror movie.

From inside the room, we were able to see the entrance to the house. There were no doors leading to the main floor, only a hatch that went down to the basement. But not the main part of the basement either. He had to climb through the root cellar then between some shelving.

It was cleverly hidden. Even with the root cellar completely devoid of junk, the only thing remaining in the room was a nearly burnt-out candle. That probably should've been a hint something was up because no other place in the house was clear of crap. No indication of the entrance could be seen unless you knew it was there, and then it jumped out at you. Had we not climbed out of the room via said entrance, it might never have been found.

The room itself was very different from the others. Maybe not at first glance since it was piled high with junk. But a closer look told a different story. Half the room was carefully packed. It wasn't boxes full of clothing and knick knacks all just haphazardly thrown in. The other side of the room was filled with guns and ammunition—a lot of guns. And not just hunting rifles. There were handguns, semi automatics, and some weapons I didn't even recognize. Around here, a collection of hunting rifles would've been nothing.

But this was both unusual and creepy, and it only got creepier as we opened the boxes.

"Look here." Leo stood hunched over a box, papers in his hand. "These are all conspiracy magazines and clippings."

What had we stumbled into? I stepped away from the guns and looked at what he was holding up. Print-offs, clippings, and entire magazines including grocery store gossip rags, and all of them had one theme: Cancer was biological warfare used to bring forth the New World Order.

This wasn't a half-assed attempt of going off-grid or being a prepper. This wasn't someone in a militia. This was the result of someone hurting and trying to make sense of the world. Clarence was farther over the deep end than any of us had suspected, and looking at his hurt piled in boxes like that, made me actually feel bad for the guy.

I still didn't, nor would I ever, forgive him for what he did to Xander and his dogs, but the hurt he felt was palpable.

"Do you think he snapped when his wife died of cancer?" Leo asked, setting the papers down.

"Or maybe before. She may not have loved him as much, or maybe she did." I never understood their relationship, but I also came in at the tail end when she was already sick. "I'm not one to judge."

"August told me about how he...when he found out Xander wasn't his biological son." He didn't say more than that. He didn't need to. His heart was huge and empathy poured off him.

I didn't know what more to say either. "Yeah."

"What do we do with all this?" He changed the subject, which was good. There was nothing to be gained by trying to figure out the dead, not when their death might very well have saved others if the arsenal we were looking at was any indication of what could have happened.

"We're gonna have to call my boss." I sighed. It was the last thing I wanted to do. "Sheriff Martin had an affinity for Clarence for some reason, and this might hurt him." And one thing Sheriff Martin was not good with was dealing with his emotions. I'd seen more than one ticket take longer than it should because someone pushed his buttons.

And this might just do that. This was going to cause problems I didn't want to deal with. But there was no other option.

"Should we carry this stuff out?" Leo folded over the flaps of the box.

"We should probably leave it as is." If I was on duty, I would have. But I was there as a friend...potential date...helper...whatever it was. I wasn't there as the town Deputy Sheriff. And really, with something like this, it was outside my training. This was a lot of guns. *Please don't let this be a Call-in-the-Feds kinda thing.*

"This was not how I expected to spend my day." Leo wiped his brow then put his hands on his hips. "At least I can look back on it and say it wasn't boring."

"It wasn't boring before all this." I needed to step up my flirting game. My words were coming out more creepy than sexy...or maybe it was the room we were in. I preferred to believe that.

He smirked. "Behind you."

I spun around, half expecting to see something crawling toward me. "What am I looking at?" As far as I could tell, the two living things in the room were both human.

"That chest, the one slightly to your left. It's different."

My eyes immediately found it, and he was right. It was different. Unlike the cardboard boxes and the fire boxes that filled the room, this one was ornate—fancy, even. I stepped over to it and slid it from its spot. "I think maybe it's a music box." I tried to flip open the lid, but couldn't. "It's locked."

"I know you're a cop or whatever, and it's your job to say no, but I think we need to open this." Leo reached into the tool box in the entryway and handed me an awl. "It feels like it doesn't belong here."

"Who's to say we didn't open it before seeing the guns?" I took it from him and managed to open the box without too much trouble. It was filled with jewelry. Most of it, if not all of it, was costume jewelry, but some of it had some age to it.

"Her jewelry." Leo ran his hand over a glass pendant. "Can I?" he asked as his hands brushed the knob of the music box.

I gave a nod, eager to hear it.

He spun the knob and not a click was heard. He spun it the other way and still nothing. "There's no resistance. No gears."

"Just a second. I think I've seen one of these." It was in a training video about drug busts, but still. I reached in and pulled the velvet up in one corner. Sure enough, there was a little bit sticking out just a tad too high. I pressed it and the top, where the music components would be held, snapped open.

Inside were folded-up papers. All of them with one word written on them. *Xander*

"What's going to happen if your boss gets these?" Leo asked.

"He'll impound them." I shut the lid. "I'll give him the rest of the stuff, so these don't wind up as evidence." Some days it was easier than others not to let the world know how much I hated my boss. But at the end of the day, I loved my job and made a difference, so it was a necessary evil.

"Didn't we find these in the bedroom with her other things?" he asked with a wink.

"I think so, and there's no reason anything from there would need to be in evidence.

Leo smiled. "Help me get these to Xander?"

"Absolutely."

We tucked the box away where it wouldn't be easily noticed, but also not hidden in a way that might draw suspicion. Then we called my boss.

So much for a hot pancake date with the new guy.

SEVEN

LEO

Five minutes after the sheriff showed up, I knew we'd made the right decision in keeping the jewelry box from him. He had already earned the name Sheriff Asshat in my head.

His first round of questions were about cash. "Find any money? Did you look for any liquid assets? I'm surprised none of the boxes held his rainy day funds." As if the house shouted money. Quite the opposite. It shouted poverty and the value of the guns was the shocking bit.

I had no doubt in my mind that he would've taken that jewelry and found some way to add it to the precinct's coffers. I'd seen a documentary on that kind of seizure, and given how small the town was, I connected those dots.

Then again, maybe I watched too much television. He was probably just a jerk on a power trip, looking at a big-deal case to earn him more praise from his followers.

In any case, he was a certifiable asshat.

"I'm sure this is nothing, but I guess we need to run it through," he finally said. For a man who spent an hour asking weird leading questions, *nothing* didn't sound quite right. "You know, just so I don't have the Feds up our asses." He went on rambling and muttering about stupid laws and the government thinking they knew how to run things better than he did.

I just stood against the wall, hoping not to be noticed.

When I pictured today, I thought I would spend it trying not to jump Ron. And for the first part of the day, that was pretty accurate. He would look up from something he was doing and give this sweet little smile that had my heart aflutter. It was more than just the physical attraction, although...whoa, that was definitely there. But yeah, it was more. He had a kindness to him I rarely saw in people.

And I certainly never pictured the day including a trip from the sheriff to share the huge gun cache we found in the secret lair of a crazy man. But here we were, doing just that.

The only good things about the location of the guns was that the man hadn't been able to easily access them. Not that I put much trust in his decision-making skills, but getting to them required going into the root cellar and up a hidden staircase and back down again.

My heart went out to the poor kid who had lived here. I hadn't met him yet, but from what August, Jase, and Ron had said, and the way their faces all softened as they spoke of him, he was a pretty great kid.

I was looking forward to getting his mother's things to him. It sucked that in a small town like this, there was no way he wouldn't hear about the craziness that was his father—or the man he thought was his father. But that would probably be true in the city as well.

After loading the guns, the sheriff seemed to think of a thousand more questions he needed to ask me. For a minute, I thought he was going to accuse me of being the one to stash them. And really, if Ron hadn't been with me when they were found, I had no doubt I'd have been handcuffed and in the back of his car already.

But if I was going to be handcuffed, there was only one officer I wanted to have that pleasure...and it would be in the bedroom.

He finally made a noise like he was going to leave. Thank goodness. Maybe Ron would agree to have those pancakes with me for dinner. Too bad I couldn't use the kitchen yet. The thought of syrup led to so many possibilities, none of them appropriate to be thinking about in this situation.

He tapped on his clipboard. "Now about the camper... Whose is it?"

"It's mine. I'm using it while I finish gutting the house." It was less than ideal, at least until I got more water, but it worked.

Jase and August said I could use the shower at their house as needed, and bottled water was enough for most other things. It was better than driving all the way to a hotel in town at the end of the day.

He started writing as if I'd said something important. After making a scribbled mess, he tore off the paper and handed it to me.

"Thank you," I said automatically, not looking at it immediately. My eyes were glued behind him to Ron. For some reason, his jaw had just dropped.

The sheriff grunted. "You better have that paid on time."

Paid? On time? What was he talking about? How could I be fined for the guns? I just found them...and then I looked down at what I now knew to be a citation —a citation for the camper. What the fuck? "It's temporary."

He glared at my response.

And because I'm so brilliant, I kept going. "It's only here while I work on the house."

"Doesn't matter." He scolded like I was a child. "Can't be here. City Ordinance states that camping is only to be done in nonresidential zones and campers only by permit. We can't have riff raff here, thinking they can do what they want." He made it very clear I was said riff raff.

"Move it." He snapped the clipboard to his side. "It needs to be undercover and uninhabited while stored on the property. Until such a time as you can prove that it fits the criteria for a residence, the town won't be able to issue a permit to place it on this land. And don't even bother trying until you have a plan for electricity and water."

"Yes, sir." There was no point arguing with him. Not when he made his disdain for me so obvious. Apparently, he didn't appreciate my audacity in discovering a crime.

I wasn't sure what I was going to do. A hotel room would be both expensive and a pain in the ass, adding time to my rebuild, since that was what this project was turning in to.

All I did know was that I didn't want to mess with him.

"I think we can get the board—" Ron tried to offer a solution but he was cut off with a hand.

I still appreciated his effort in making things better.

"I'll move it," I reassured them both, not wanting Ron to deal with the fallout simply because he was helping me.

"Oh, you better." The sheriff stared me down, trying to further intimidate me. "I'll be checking, and if I see it out here again and it's not covered or it's showing any signs of inhabitation, it'll be impounded and this fine will look like peanuts." He turned and stormed off, done with the conversation.

Ron looked appalled. "I'm sorry about that. I didn't know he was going to pull that shit. If I did, I'd have had us move it first."

As if I would blame him for his asshole boss. I understood why they had the rule. No one wants people squatting on land, but that was hardly the case here. He could've let it go. He just didn't want to. Asshat.

"Maybe you can help me find one of those rooms you were talking about?" I shrugged it off like it wasn't making my blood boil. It wasn't as if he had anything to do with it.

"You don't need to do that. You can stay at my place." He made the offer like it was no big deal. "I've got plenty of room, and it's my fault he came here in the first place." It definitely wasn't. "I should've anticipated that shitstorm, so I kind of blame myself."

"Is he always such an..."

"Dick? Yep. Always."

"How do you work for him—day in and day out?"
There was no way I could deal with someone like that
on a regular basis.

"Because he's the only part of my job I don't like. I love
the people in town. I love helping. I love serving." He
shrugged. "Really, the only thing I don't love is him, and
in theory, come election day, he could be voted out."

"What do you mean 'in theory'?" Was small-town
corruption a real thing? I needed to stop with the television, which would be easy given my current
situation.

"Seeing as no one's actually ever run against him, the
chances are slim."

I never quite understood why sheriffs were elected offi-
cials, but then again, I grew up in a pride where the
hierarchy was set in place. After that, I was in the city
where we had police chiefs instead of sheriffs.

"How come you haven't run?" I couldn't imagine
anyone who had met them both not wanting to vote
for Ron.

"Because I'd like to keep my job. I don't want to run, lose, and end up not able to do what I love."

"Are you sure about me staying with you? I promise it'll only be a couple days until I can figure all this out." Maybe the permit thing wasn't the huge obstacle he made it out to be.

"I'm sure, and it doesn't have to be a couple days. It's about time I had a roommate. It gets kind of lonely."

I understood that too well. At least I had my cat. It wasn't quite the same, though. Sometimes you just wanted another person to talk to.

Mate.

Someone who wasn't a bossy cat thinking they knew everything.

"In that case, I accept." It would be a huge relief to have a place to stay with running water, and as long as I kept my hands to myself, I'd be fine. I should've answered *Challenge Accepted* because that was the only snafu in this entire plan.

"Oh, what about your cat? He hasn't been around today." He started looking around as if expecting to find a kitty hiding in a corner somewhere. "I hope he's okay."

Shit. I'd forgotten about my "pet" cat. "Oh, right..."

"Damn...you can't bring him to my place. I forgot about that." He rubbed his chin. "My landlady has one rule and pets are it."

"You know what? It's okay." I took out my phone and dialed Jase, so glad we had met. He picked up on the first ring. "Hey, Jace. I was wondering if you could do me a huge favor." I stepped away, pretending I was looking for a stronger signal, which wasn't untrue either. This place didn't do well with my provider.

"What's up?"

"The sheriff said I can't use my trailer anymore, so I was hoping you might be able to catsit for me." The phone went silent and then I heard him relaying the story to August.

"August agrees on one condition. When you get here to drop him off, you have to tell us every last detail." He was barely containing his laughter.

"Yeah, yeah. I'll be there after we move the trailer. Thanks."

Ron helped me put a tarp over the camper then he went home to get cleaned up while I gathered the cat and dropped him off. He made sure to mention getting my pet fixed, not knowing he had already told me that and it was a hard no. But I couldn't be upset by the suggestion. His heart was in the right place. That didn't stop my balls from shrivelling up.

The laughter August had contained over the phone was definitely not contained once I pulled up their drive. They were cracking up before I got out of the car, and how they managed not to choke on their cookies as I told them about Ron being on a mission to have my cat neutered was beyond me.

"I'm glad you find this so funny." I grabbed another cookie because if they were going to have such a good time listening to my story, they could pay me in sugar.

"It's only funny because my mate was my pet first too." August winked at Jase.

I scoffed and almost choked on my mouthful. "I never said he was my mate."

"Don't have to...your cat did." August shrugged. "How are you even holding him in?"

Damn. They could see it. My cat could see it. And as much as I didn't want to see it, I saw it too. "But he's human."

August just shook his head. As a human, he didn't buy that lame excuse. "Try again."

"You really think Ron, the human deputy, is my mate?" I spoke as much to them as to myself.

How was that even possible?

EIGHT

RON

"What was I thinking?" I mumbled to myself on the way back to my place. First, I invited a complete stranger to move in with me. Granted, I was partially to blame for him needing a house in the first place. But then I threw my address at him and practically ran out of there, leaving him to find his cat and deal with him on his own.

If it had been anybody else, I'd have probably done the same thing, at least as far as offering a place to stay. But with Leo it was different. He was someone I had already tried to get on a date, someone I was trying to impress. Bringing him into my home had "bad decision" written all over it.

I pulled into my parking spot and sprinted toward the door. The house was clean enough but definitely not company ready. Plus, I stank. Ripping apart walls and going through moldy crap had a way of doing that.

I started with a shower, not feeling clean enough to do all the other things that needed doing. After getting washed up, I threw on some clothes and scrambled around the house, trying to make it look like I was neater than I was. Finally, I went to the spare bedroom and put new sheets on the bed. It had been a long time since anybody stayed in the room, and while the sheets were clean, they weren't fresh and crisp.

I shouldn't have been trying to impress the stranger-turned-friend. But I was doing exactly that. In a way, it was good. It kept me from focusing on the shitstorm that was Clarence's hidden armory. We all knew Clarence wasn't an ideal parent, and I tried my best to look out for Xander when I could. But I'd also seen the broken system, the one that would have a social worker drive in from too far away and claim nothing was wrong so they wouldn't have to make the trip again. In most cases, the scare was enough to get parents on the right track. In Xander's case, I had a feeling his life would've spiraled deeper into hell with any more overt intervention.

At the time, I understood grief played a part in the way he acted. I just didn't understand how deep that went. But that didn't explain his dive into conspiracy-theory, gun-hoarding territory. People lost spouses every day. It was awful, but it was a part of life. I couldn't imagine the pain of going through a loss like that, but I liked to think I was strong enough to not have it mold me into some kind of psychopath.

Never had I thought the day would come that I felt bad for the man.

The guns, though—that had me nervous. There was no way he got them all legally...not in this state and with his finances. I hoped that when the serial numbers were run, a logical explanation of how he acquired them was as bright as a neon sign. The last thing this town needed was the Feds poking around and bringing negative attention to us. As it was, we still had daily calls about the factory that was potentially trying to set up shop. This would be four thousand times worse.

I took out the vacuum because the need to make the place as presentable as it could be was pushing at me. He was coming from a place we couldn't dream of walking around barefoot in without a tetanus shot, and

I wanted my already-clean carpets to be cleaner. I was clearly a wreck, but he deserved it.

Leo's day had gone to shit.

I still didn't understand what made Martin think he could just go in there and be an asshole like he owned the world. I mean, he did it because he could get away with it, obviously, but the reasoning for it perplexed me. Writing a ticket like that was just a dick move. Yeah, sure, it was technically the ordinance, but no one cared about a temporary RV on a guy's personal property. They especially wouldn't care in this instance. From the looks of things, we were lucky that place hadn't gone up in flames long ago. Really, Leo was most likely saving the town's volunteer fire department a bunch of risk.

Besides, the ordinance was set up to avoid people squatting on other people's land. It wasn't intended to make it hard for people to fix up their homes. It was ridiculous to even insinuate that it was.

It wasn't even like it was an eyesore. No one could see the house as they traveled down the long dirt road to the center of town. Maybe if it was in town, I could understand keeping properties free of blight. But where he was, there shouldn't have been any issue. It was all a power trip, an *I'm important* with a little *fuck you city guy* on the side. Nothing more.

I'm not sure if me being there helped or not. It kept Leo from being brought in on gun charges, but it obviously didn't help him out of the ticket. Maybe that was the sheriff's way of getting back at me for helping the *riff raff*. He never understood the concept of being kind to others when you didn't get something in return. It drove him crazy when people smiled and waved at me while I was out of uniform.

As I shut off the vacuum, I decided to also shut off the noise in my head. There was no changing any of it, so there was no reason to let it get to me.

I put the vacuum away and took the laundry to the washer.

The house was basically ready for Leo, but I wished I could have allowed him to bring his cat too. If Mrs. Parker wasn't so adamant about them, I might've been willing to break the rules. But that was the one thing she was hardcore about. No cats or dogs allowed. I imagined it included bunnies and rats too, but I never mentioned those.

I was already in love with Leo's cat and was disappointed I hadn't gotten to see him all day. I could've kicked myself for that comment about neutering him, though. The way Leo almost turned green at the suggestion made me realize I was being a little preachy. I wasn't wrong that it was best for the cat and the community, but my delivery had obviously upset him.

Thankfully, he had met Jase and August already. Their grounds were pretty much where all animals who needed some extra loving wound up. The cat would have fun there unless he pissed off Lux. Lux ruled that place even though Daisy thought she did.

August and Jase were good people, and I was happy Leo was already forging a friendship with them. Being new in a small town held different challenges than in the city. When I moved in, I was the new guy for six years.

I considered putting a pot of water on to boil but then thought better of it. We already had noodles for lunch. Granted they were instant noodles from a cup, but they were noodles nonetheless. Another pasta dish was probably the last thing he wanted to eat. Since that was pretty much the extent of my culinary expertise, we had to consider a plan B.

Maybe our dinner date could still happen if he wasn't too exhausted from the day. Worst-case scenario, I could order take-away. It wouldn't be as good, but it would still be better than spaghetti.

The knock on the door made me smile. I couldn't help it. There was just something about Leo that made my body tingle. But that's not all there was to it. There was a connection between us, one I'd never felt before. It was odd and beautiful and scary and so many things all at once. It was like a first crush on steroids. And while it probably wouldn't last, I planned on enjoying it for now.

When I swung open the door, my smile fell. Standing before me was Sheriff Asshat. I schooled my face, not wanting to make things worse than the scowl on his face suggested they were.

"What's up, Sheriff?" I stood in front of the open door, blocking it. I didn't want him to come in, but also didn't want him to feel he couldn't. It was a fine line.

"You think that troublemaker brought those guns?"

"I'm pretty sure he didn't, sir." As in of course he fucking didn't.

"And how do you know?"

As if we hadn't already gone over that. "Because I helped him take down the moldy paneling, and we opened up the room for the first time."

"Yeah, well, maybe he put that paneling up."

Was he insane or mean or both? "Sir, he didn't. It had been there for a long time."

He crossed his arms over his chest and leaned on my door jamb. "I don't see Clarence being into that stuff. I just don't."

Ah, okay. I finally got it. At least I thought I did. The sheriff didn't want to think his friend was into that level of wackadoodle. "Maybe he didn't, but that doesn't mean that the new guy did." If giving Clarence the benefit of the doubt helped him sleep at night, so be it.

"I don't trust this new city guy."

"I see that, sir. Did you run the serial numbers?" There were a lot so I doubted he got them all, but chances were they would have similar results.

"Most of the ones that came back were sold at shows." That wasn't unusual but the sheer volume of weaponry is what needed a closer look. Especially considering all the papers he had full of conspiracy shit.

"So, where do we go from here?" I dreaded the answer, not wanting to deal with state or federal officers coming in and taking over. But I was pretty sure that would be his answer.

"He needs to come in for more questions," he barked.

"I'm pretty sure he doesn't know anything." Leo knew even less than I did so continuing to ask him questions was a waste of everyone's time. Not to mention that this conversation shouldn't be happening at my front door, but I wasn't going to invite him in.

"Clarence was a lot of things, and I heard the rumors. People didn't like him. But this was not his doing. Bring him in or I will."

I nodded, knowing I had no other option. "I'll bring him in tomorrow. He's planning on working on the house again." The sheriff didn't need to know his potential suspect was on his way over to sleep in my bed. Not *my* bed but close enough to make the sheriff even more hostile if he knew.

"Be sure you do." He stomped off.

I needed to see what those results really said. If he thought he could somehow pin anything on Leo, there was something more than buying guns for cash going on.

NINE
LEO

The guys were still teasing me when I finally took off for Ron's address. He lived in an adorable little house. It was more of a cottage, complete with window boxes. I could easily picture a grandmother owning it more than the town deputy, but in an odd way, it suited him. I climbed out with the small bag I'd packed in hand, anxious and nervous to get inside. Fortunately, I'd showered over at Jase's, so at least I wasn't bringing the dirt and stink of the day with me.

August's comment about his mate being his pet first really got to me. He was human. And I knew that before, but it really sank in today. The idea was troublesome, and I needed to process it. Although once I walked into Ron's house, with his scent permeating the place, chances were good I wouldn't be able to think of much other than him...preferably naked.

It wasn't like I could just go up to him and say, "Hey, guess what? I'm your mate, but lions don't have human mates, and really I'm a cat not a lion, so help me figure this out."

Even if I wanted to woo him in the way humans seemed to live for, there was the little problem of me staying at his house. The timing was truly shit, and it was best to just keep it in my pants.

August swore Ron would be fine with my secret if I chose to share it. After all, he and Jase were happy. Except this wasn't the same thing. August had bonded with his bunny before meeting human Jase. And then there was the whole Jase leaving thing that still perplexed me. How could a mate leave, even for a day?

But still, the evidence of their love surrounded them. They were the real deal.

Gah. This mate thing was hard—almost as hard as I was pretty much nonstop.

I stepped up to the doorway, raised my hand to knock, and he opened the door, his hair still damp.

"Come on in." Ron stepped out of my way to let me inside.

I brushed by him, needing that slight touch and instantly feeling guilty by it. *Things would be so much easier if he were a shifter.*

"I was going to make us some dinner." He pointed to a pot on the stove. "But then I realized, I only know how to cook spaghetti, or some variation of that." His cheeks turned a slight color pink. *Adorable.*

"No worries." I was hungry, but he was already doing enough for me without having to cook. "Wait, want to walk down to get pancakes? If you're up for it, I mean." I was so freaking smooth—like sandpaper smooth.

"Yeah, I'd like that." He grabbed his keys off the hook on the wall and slid them into his pocket.

Maybe this wouldn't be so hard. Maybe he felt it too. *Or maybe he was being nice, and I was overreading things.*

I lifted the bag in my hand. "Where do you want me to… "

"Oh, sorry." He grabbed it and let out a long breath. "I'll show you to your room." He led me down a small corridor and past what I assumed to be his room which shared a wall with the one I was going to be using.

He set my bag down on the twin bed. The enclosed space gave me a very real feel of how rough things were going to be for me while I stayed there. His scent was enveloping me, my cat was pouncing at me to make a move, and I had to position my hand in just the right way to hide my boner. His scent of sunshine and rainbows sounded so cliche but there was no better way to describe it. Damn, I wanted to rub against him. Or maybe that was the cat being pushy. This was going to be hard and wonderful....and hard.

"It's not much." He slipped his hands in his pockets and looked around the room. "But I hope it'll do."

"I can't tell you how much I appreciate this." Even if he wasn't my mate, this kindness to someone he barely knew...it meant a lot. He treated me better than my pride after my first shift, and I had a feeling it wasn't just me specifically. Ron was just a kind man. "At least let me pay rent." It was the least I could do.

"Don't be ridiculous. That's what neighbors do." He smiled and patted my shoulder. "They help each other."

Prides were supposed to do that too, but here we were.

"I'm hardly your neighbor. I live miles down the road."

He laughed. "In a town like this, that's a neighbor."

"To a city boy, a neighbor is someone whose apartment you can see from your doorway." Not that I knew any of mine. Where I used to live, everyone stuck to themselves. It was fine, I guess. This definition of neighbor, though? I liked it much better.

"It's a good thing you're not in the city anymore. You'd have no neighbors."

Something was off, but I couldn't quite put my finger on it. Then again, just because I was feeling an insane connection to him didn't mean he was anything toward me. And anything I said at that point would just come across as weird.

The situation was weird enough without me adding more weirdness to it.

The walk to the diner ended up being much shorter than I thought it would. That was good for my belly but not for getting enough air to not be bombarded with his scent the second we stepped inside. The diner was everything a small town diner should be, complete with shiny chrome and bright red booths.

People were sitting in most of the seats, including those at the counter, but Ron and I were lucky enough to get a booth with some privacy.

"I'm good to see ya!" I had no idea what that meant as a cute little thing from behind the counter called out to Ron. She waved and a huge smile showed her perfect teeth.

He smiled back and said the same to her.

Great. I picked the one guy in town who was straight, or at least interested in a woman. A stunning one at that. Damn, my green eyes of jealousy popped out fast. I needed to pipe that down. It didn't have a place to stay without him, so even if he was with her, I had no say in it.

We sat down, and she came bouncing over with two glasses of water. "Hey, Ron. See you brought the new guy."

Apparently, that was going to be my name for years, according to Jase. He said the only reason he wasn't the new guy anymore was because I moved to town. *Glad to be of service.*

"Camille, this is Leo." He set his hand on mine briefly and then acted like he was reaching for something. It was all my cat needed to calm down. He wasn't even a shifter, and yet somehow he knew I needed reassurance. Or maybe he was making a move. Either worked for me. "He just moved here from *the city*. He's fixing up Clarence's old place, and I've been helping."

She let out a whistle. "Oh, you got a lot of work cut out for you."

"Definitely." And she didn't know the half of it. "Nice to meet you." Now that my cat had calmed down, it was the truth.

"Guessin' you're here for the pancakes."

"I've been told they're the best, and you even have the good stuff to pour over them."

"You better be talking about the real syrup or else I might need to take back my first impression of you."

She scribbled my order on her notepad, not even bothering to ask Ron his.

"You think I'd bring anyone here who didn't?" Ron winked at me, and while it was a general wink and probably more to punctuate his joke, I held on to it like it meant something more.

She took our drink orders too then bounced back to the food window. Seriously, she bounced. The energy flying off her was kinetic. I could use just a fraction of it after the day I had.

I watched her until she disappeared into the kitchen. "She seems nice."

"Oh, she is." Ron offered me a straw, and I took it just for something to do with my hands. "She and her husband took over this place a couple years back. They've been doing a really good job. It's hard for a restaurant to survive in a town like this. People don't go out to eat as much as they do in the city, and when they do, it's usually just people like me coming in to buy their one order of pancakes."

She was married. My shoulders relaxed at that. I was officially a hot mess.

We chatted while we ate the most delicious pancakes I'd ever tasted. Then we chatted some more. And just because we could, we ended our meal with some banana cream.

For the entire meal, Ron sat across from me all confident and sexy. I, on the other hand, sat there trying not to squirm in my seat, my pants way too tight.

If it was this bad in a restaurant, what was it going to be like when we were home later tonight?

Maybe he'd let me turn off the air conditioning and open up the window.

That would help my cat quiet down and wouldn't seem too odd. Right? Everyone does that.

Dinner was wonderful. I hadn't laughed or had so much fun in a long time. And even with our very different backgrounds, we had a lot in common. We talked about how we both enjoy reading, although I prefer my sci-fi to his fantasy. And we'd both rather play a sport than watch it on television. Randomly, both of us said our favorite color was green. And less randomly, we're both painfully single. That last part I may have embellished on. I was painfully single and he had just said single. I still took it as a good sign.

As we reached home, Leo's exhaustion started to take over. He'd been sleeping in a camper and had been emptying the house for a lot longer than I had. It was a miracle the poor guy was still standing.

I offered him a cup of tea, but he politely excused himself to get some rest. Had I not seen the bags under his eyes and his pace slowing on the way home, I might've thought it was me that had him racing off to bed.

But I truly believed he just needed to sleep.

Which was the excuse I gave myself for not telling him he was going to have to deal with the sheriff in the morning. He wouldn't be able to relax with that over his head. And it wasn't like knowing tonight would change anything.

Once I was alone, I turned on the television and flipped through the channels, trying to find something to distract me from the sexiness in the next room. As expected, nothing did.

Then I got an idea. I knocked on his door to let him know I needed to go to work for a bit, and then I left. The tug to stay was real. It couldn't be healthy to be so attracted and connected to someone this soon. Not that I had any say in the matter.

I walked into work, glad to see Sheriff Martin had left for the day. With the way he was earlier, I was afraid he would still be there.

It didn't take me long to realize he had done jack shit as far as paperwork went. Not logging things into the computer. Not even a paper list on his desk. Nothing. Was he so desperate to keep the Feds away that he was willing to skip protocols all together?

But that wasn't right. He said he ran the serial numbers, right?

I went to find the guns. Maybe I couldn't find his paper trail, but I could at least look the records up myself. Something was up. I just needed to figure out what.

It took me a while to find them. Not all of them, but some of them. They were in a random box with no label. None. Everything in that room needed to be labelled. It was the rule of crossing the threshold, and yet not one gun had a label and the box was blank.

I took some photos of a few serial numbers. I didn't want to disturb things too much, but I couldn't leave without some information. Back at my desk, I started looking them up in the database. Not all of them were there, but a few matched and proved he was right. Those were sold via private sales. Of course, it wasn't easy to search, which was intentional and a pain in the ass in cases like this.

All of that was good and normal. What wasn't normal were the two guns that showed up not as sales, but as being confiscated by this station...and neither of them were under Clarence's name. One was taken from the scene of a speeding ticket gone wrong and the other was found by the river. Neither was ever claimed. In theory, they should still be sitting in the back with identification tags on them.

Clearly, they were not.

I deleted everything I found and then shut down my computer. I couldn't deal with any of this right now, at least not here. I took a few minutes to fill out some reports for some random calls that didn't result in anything significant so I had some plausible reason for being there so late.

I wasn't sure exactly what was up, but this helped explain why the sheriff was such a jerk about that room. He was scared of something but what? That was still to be determined. All I knew was that somehow, he was connected to those weapons.

If not, his actions made no sense. Filing a report saying the crazy dead guy had guns shouldn't have been a big deal. It wasn't like the town didn't already know some-thing had been off about the guy.

But I needed to get home. No, I wanted to be home. I turned off the lights and locked up.

There was something about the stranger, who didn't feel like a stranger, that had me needing to be there with him, even if I was still a room away. The word that bounced around in my head every time things got quiet was *home*. He felt like home which was weird and insane, and I didn't even understand it. But there it was, and no part of me wanted to fight it.

I liked the guy—a lot—and from the way he got jealous of Camille, he liked me too.

The entire trip back to my house, the word kept repeating over and over again. *Home. Home. Home.* I shook it off as I reached the front door and then adjusted my jeans. At least he was in bed. If not, there was no way he wouldn't notice the bulge in my jeans.

I turned the knob quietly, not wanting to wake him up. When I opened the door, I was totally startled because he wasn't in bed. He was on the couch, his pajama pants tented.

Great. We were both hard. Nothing embarrassing about that.

"Hi." He pulled his bottom lip in with his teeth.

"Sorry, I had some paperwork to do. I hope I didn't wake you." *He's sitting up on the couch, dumbass. Obviously, I did!*

He sighed. "I can't sleep."

"Do you want some tea?" Tea was the thing you offered, right? Angeline always did. Not that this situation was anything like any of the times I was at her place.

He shook his head.

"Wine makes you sleepy, but all I have is beer? You want a beer?"

He shook his head again.

"Um, maybe some warm milk?" I was running out of ideas and only managed to make an awkward situation even more awkward.

"I was thinking maybe we could talk." He shrugged and looked up at me, his vulnerability shining bright in his eyes.

Talk. I could talk. Possibly not coherently with the way my cock was pressing against my jeans, but words could be formed.

"Yeah, of course." I sat beside him on the couch, the only furniture I had in the room. "What's up?"

He took a deep breath and exhaled before speaking. "I want you."

His bluntness had me second-guessing my ears. "Okay." What else could I say to that?

"If you want me to leave, I understand, but I just." He buried his face in his hands for a moment then looked back at me. "I don't know. I felt I should tell you."

He was so stinkin' adorable like this. "I want you too." I put my hand on his thigh, jealous of his pants for being able to touch his skin. Rational thought had clearly left the building. "But please don't think you need to... Well, just so you know, this is not a condition of...you can still..."

His lips slammed into mine, ending my word vomit and stealing my breath away.

AFTER KISSING RON HARD ENOUGH THAT WE WERE both gasping for air, I couldn't wait any longer. My human mind was telling me to slow down and give it some more time. But my cat was horny and ready and there wasn't any stopping him. Frankly, I was pretty horny too, and I couldn't let this opportunity pass me by.

I slipped my hand across his chest and let it slide down to his waist. "May I?"

He nodded as he adjusted his position on the couch so I was lying above him. Once he was relaxed and staring up at me, I flicked the button on his jeans and slipped my fingers inside. He was hard and pressing up against the zipper, begging me to reach in and take hold of him. I wasn't one to make a man beg, especially not someone I wanted as badly as I wanted Ron, so I released his zipper and pulled out his cock.

Ron lifted his hips, pressing into my grip as he moaned softly. "Yes, Leo. Please."

"Anything." I pushed up his shirt and dragged my tongue down his firm chest, circling his nipples before venturing lower. When I was within tasting distance of his cock, all my primal desires came forth, and I couldn't slow things down. I opened my lips and sucked in his smooth head, savoring the tangy flavor that filled my mouth. "Mmm."

"Oh, god." He slid his fingers through my hair and held me in place. "If you keep humming like that, I'm gonna come."

I smiled around him as I slid up and down his shaft, learning every vein and ridge in his thick girth. "I want you to."

He closed his eyes and threw his head back as he fucked my mouth. I bobbed up and down, pulling off him as his balls tightened, afraid he'd come too soon.

When he caught his breath, his finger traveled around my thigh and tapped at my opening. I was wet and fluttering as he easily slipped inside me. He pumped me slowly, but slowly was not what I needed. I scooted around so he had access to my ass, and I could still reach his cock. Then I swallowed him down, wanting to taste his offering.

"Leo!"

As soon as he pushed up and his entire body went rigid, I knew he was ready. Ron unloaded into my mouth and down my throat. "Fuck!"

"Give it to me," I said with a mouthful of his cream dripping from the corners of my mouth. "I want it."

He did, filling me with his come as my cat begged me to fully claim him as ours.

After he relaxed against the couch, he pulled me forward and captured my lips with his, taking some of his own flavor into his mouth while we shifted positions so I was underneath him. "Now I need you inside me..."

I loved that he wanted to be in control, giving me what I wanted so badly. While we kissed, we managed to free ourselves of the rest of our clothes until we were both naked and sweaty against each other.

I sat up and tilted my hips so his cock rubbed along my crack, lubing up with my natural arousal. "It's been a while."

"I'll be gentle." His hands slid down my back and cupped my ass. Ron pulled my cheeks apart then slid two fingers in, stretching me so I could take him.

"God, that feels good. I think I'm ready." I sat straight up and positioned my opening above his cock then slowly lowered down onto his dick, sucking him inside me. "I need this, Ron."

"Me too, babe." He pressed up and closed the small gap between us until we were skin to skin again, his shaft fully buried inside my channel.

After a deep breath, I started moving up and down, riding him with our eyes locked the entire time. I couldn't remember ever feeling more complete than I did with him.

Our pace quickened, and I could feel his knot beginning to form. "I want you to knot me."

His teeth pressed against my shoulder, almost hard enough to break the skin, to mark me.

"Yessss!" I cried out, my cat fully ready to reciprocate.

His head snapped back and the moment was lost, but my mind was already elsewhere as he slammed into my prostate, sending stars across my vision as my cock prepared to explode.

I started moving faster, pushing us both toward the goal we were so desperate for. "Yes."

With that one word, Ron's fingers closed around my hips and he held me in place.

I came, shooting onto his bare chest and belly as he filled me with his knot and his seed, locking it and himself inside me. "Fuck, that was good."

He rubbed my back and kissed my forehead. "It was perfect. Just like you."

TWELVE
RON

Waking up alone sucked.

I understood why he snuck out in the dead of night. Why wouldn't he? We barely knew each other, and it wasn't like we'd really talked about things. Going to bed with someone is one thing...waking up with them is another.

I climbed out of bed, trying not to have a pity party for one. Sleeping in the other room was hardly rejection. *Then why did it sting?*

After a quick trip to the bathroom, I padded into the kitchen to make some coffee. It hadn't finished brewing when Leo came out, his pajama pants low on his hips and no shirt. Gah. A man could get used to that.

"Morning." I held up two coffee cups and raised an eyebrow.

"Definitely." He came around the counter and took a seat. "Your boss sent a text and said I'm not allowed on the property until the investigation is complete." He let out a long sigh.

I guess that meant he didn't want him to go in for questioning. If he had, he'd have mentioned it. That man needed to get his head on straight. Besides, he had no authority to do that. At this point, there was no crime. Just a stash of guns. It seemed suspicious, but at least Leo didn't have to waste his day dealing with questions he had no answers for.

"Oh, I'm sorry. That sucks." I poured his coffee. It looked like he wanted to play the *nothing happened last night* game, and while I wasn't into that plan, I respected his desire to do so. Things in his life were complicated enough. "What do you want to do today? I have the day off. If you need help with something else, like maybe ordering things or picking them up."

He blew into his hot mug, sending a blast of steam into the air. "I was thinking maybe we could bring the box to Doc's place?"

"That's a good idea. Xander will be in school, so it will give us some privacy." We hadn't read the letters, but I had a feeling they would strip open a lot of wounds, and Doc may want to wait until he was older to give them to Xander.

As we drove to Doc's, I kept the windows open. Ever since last night, all I wanted to do was smell him. There was something about his scent that called to me, and the longer I was surrounded by it, the harder it was to respect his space. Opening the truck windows made a huge difference, but the draw was far from gone. Not petting him...yes, petting...took a lot of concentration.

We'd given Doc a heads up we were coming but hadn't told him the details of why. It felt like the kind of thing best explained in person.

"Doc's practice is connected to his home," I said as we drove down the dirt road that led to his place. At one time, it had been a family farm, but the fields had long grown over except for the small herb garden he used for his practice. He was pretty old-fashioned like that. "It works out well because he doesn't have the packed schedules of city practices." I'd heard horror stories of people trying to get in when they were sick. Here, most of the time, all it took was a phone call.

"That's pretty cool." His hand settled on my thigh. Maybe he wasn't feeling day-after blues afterall.

I placed my hand on his as I drove into the driveway and found Doc outside, holding some herbs that looked more like weeds.

He waved to us as I opened the door. "Hey, Ron. It's good to see you." He took a step back and looked at Leo. "See you brought the new guy." He winked.

Was it that obvious? Did it matter?

"Yeah, seems to be my name around here." Leo held out his hand for Doc. "I'm Leo."

"I think August was the new guy for...I don't know...ever. And he grew up here during the summers." Doc shook his hand and chuckled. "It's the way of things."

"We brought you something." I opened up the back door and reached for the box. "We found it over at Xander's old place." It was Clarence's place to most of town, but when I was around Doc, I tried to be cognizant of the hurt his family endured over there and kept that man's name out of my conversations.

Doc had taken Xander under his wing after it all went down, and he saw far more than we ever would. "My son's at school."

My heart filled with warmth at hearing him call Xander his son.

His eyes narrowed as he looked between us. "But from the looks on your faces, that may not be a bad thing. Come on in."

We followed the doctor into his kitchen where we sat around the table, placing the chest in the center.

"We found a secret room at the house. It was mostly filled with guns, though that's currently unreleased information."

Doc rubbed his brow. "That man was crazier than a shithouse rat."

"Apparently, even more than any of us realized."

"The room was behind paneling and the entrance was hidden in the root cellar," Leo explained, turning the box to face Doc.

Doc cussed under his breath. "And this was in there?"

"This, and a bunch of guns and all sorts of crazy conspiracy shit." I placed my hand on Doc's, and when he met my eyes I added, "This was in the other room, though...of course."

He understood my meaning. "This isn't the kind of thing to be in a room like that. What's in it?"

"Mostly jewelry." Leo opened the lid. "But there's a secret box here. I'll show you." He pushed the cloth over to engage the secret lever and open the small compartment with the letters. "They're all addressed to Xander."

"Have you read them?" He reached for them, and halfway there, he pulled his hand back.

"No, we didn't have the heart to. We assume they're from his mother, and since they were addressed to Xander, we thought it was best for you to decide what to do with them."

"I don't know if I feel okay just giving them to him." He shut the lid. "Parenting is hard. On one hand, they are his. On the other, maybe they were meant for him as an adult."

"I think he would understand if you read them first." I wished I had better advice for him. "We assume they're from his mom, but if they're from his dad, does he need that toxicity in this life?"

His shoulders relaxed slightly. "No, I suppose not... Thanks, I needed that permission." He stood up and grabbed the box, taking it into another room and joining us again a minute later.

"Now on to something lighter." He clapped his hands together and turned to Leo. "Why on this green earth did you buy that dump?" Straight and to the point. The tension in the room shattered at his quip.

"I needed to get out of the city. It was just...getting to be too much."

"City life isn't for everyone," Doc agreed. "I know I couldn't live in the city. Sometimes I need to let myself go live free, if you know what I mean."

"I do indeed."

Shifter.

Another shifter.

Doc was a shifter.

Had I stumbled into some sort of a pack or something? I wasn't sure, but I needed answers. Unfortunately, with Ron beside me, it wasn't like I could just say, "Doc, what kind of shifter are you? I'm thinking fox, but I'm not sure."

So I sat there, hoping for an opportunity to slip it and grateful when Ron got up and excused himself to use the restroom.

"Cat." We didn't have time to waste so I cut to the chase.

"Otter." He nodded once and smiled.

Interestingly, I'd never met an otter before.

"Your mate doesn't know." His comment wasn't a question.

"Did Jase tell you?" They had mentioned Doc but left out the otter part.

He leaned back in his chair. "No, but they know too."

"Don't laugh, but they're currently cat sitting for me." Of course, he laughed because how could he not?

"I was trying to figure out who else you might have met. There are a few of us in town." He crossed his hands in his lap and tapped his thumbs together. "How did he know you had a cat?"

"My stupid cat ran up to him and let him hold us." He wasn't stupid, but at the time, it sure felt like it. "It was nice until he told me he was going to talk to my owner about neutering me."

Doc threw his head back in a full-on belly laugh. It was only funny to him because it wasn't his balls on the chopping block.

"What's so funny?" Ron came back in, and instead of sitting down, he stood behind me, his hands settling on my shoulders. "I leave for two seconds, and you guys have a comedy show."

"I don't even remember anymore." It wasn't too far from the truth. With his hands on me, the world fell away. I hated leaving him last night. I wanted to curl around him forever, but my cat was dangerously close to purring, and there was no way to explain that without explaining everything, and I wanted more time to figure out how to do that.

"I was telling your houseguest that we should probably establish him as a patient while he's here and I have the time." Good man. "If you want, I can drop him back at your place when we're done. I need to go to town anyway."

"Is everything okay?" His hands tightened on my shoulder, and I looked up at him. He was worried.

"Yeah. Yeah, I just...I get these weird allergies, and I didn't realize my prescription was almost gone until this morning." That sounded plausible, right? I hated lying to him even if it was something stupid. "Doc offered, and I figured I might as well since I can't go home." Which still pissed me the fuck off. The sheriff had no right to do that—probably. Again, my knowledge was based on television shows so maybe he could. Shit, maybe he could seize the property.

I sounded like I was making stuff up, which of course, I was.

"Yeah." He walked around me. "Okay, that could... That's good."

Damn, I hurt his feelings.

"But I can come back and get you, if you want." His eyes were pleading as he looked at me.

Doc waved off the idea. "I'll bring him back. I can't miss Sugar Pie Day."

From the way Ron's face turned from disappointed to childlike glee, I figured Sugar Pie Day was something amazing.

"Sugar pie what?" Although it didn't really matter since I was on board anything these men were that excited about.

"You don't know what sugar pie is?" Ron looked legitimately shocked.

I shook my head, trying to recall if I'd ever heard of it before.

Doc seemed pleased by this segue. "How about we meet in a couple hours and have ourselves some sugar pie. No man should live life without the wonders of sugar pie."

"I can't believe you've never had sugar pie." Ron took out his phone and started scrolling through. "What did the city folks do for dessert?" He handed me his phone with a picture showing.

I didn't want to burst their bubble, but it looked like custard pie to me.

"Nothing like this." I smiled and handed the phone back. "See you then?"

We all walked outside, and I waved him off before we kept up the pretense and walked to the next door, the one leading to Doc's office.

He barely had the door shut before the questions started. "So, what brought you to our little neck of the woods?"

"I guess I've been itching to get out of the city." I shrugged.

He swirled his hand, indicating he wanted more information.

"Fine." I rolled my eyes and gave him what he wanted. "People kept trying to rescue me and bring me to the shelter."

He pursed his lips, obviously struggling to keep a straight face.

"And you're about to laugh again."

"Only because it's funny." He sat on a rolly stool and pushed the receptionist's chair my way. "Sit. Stay a while."

"Thanks." I sat down, glad he found me so amusing.

"And don't pretend you don't know it's funny. You're the one who got yourself a cat sitter."

"What else could I do? Even if Ron's landlord let him have cats, it wasn't like I could be in two bodies at once." The obvious response would be to tell him the truth, but I wasn't ready for that...not yet. "He kept telling me I needed to get him fixed. He even gave me the name of a vet."

Doc nodded his head, trying to look serious. "Did you agree?"

"No! I did not. I can't even...can we move on from the Leo amuses Doc portion of the day?"

"I suppose." He stared at me in silence.

"So..." There was even more silence. I wasn't sure if he was waiting for me to just share what I wanted to share or if he was trying to figure out what to say or if he was in his head about the letters. I figured it just best to wait it out.

"The town loves you, by the way. You saved us from a factory moving in."

"That's good, I suppose. Although the sheriff hates me." And if he wasn't the sheriff, I wouldn't give a hoot. But he was, and I was found in the possession of a ton of guns so I didn't need him to hate me.

"The sheriff is a jackass. Don't be fooled into thinking the town doesn't know that. He'll get his comeuppance."

Please let that be true. How Ron put up with him on a daily basis was beyond me.

"You look like there's something you want to ask. Spit it out. I won't be late to sugar pie."

I didn't have something, I had a ton of things floating around in my head that I wanted to ask. And while Jase and August would be happy to talk to me about most of it, they were also new guys and might not know much more than I did about some things.

"Do the humans in town know about the shifters?" August did, but August was a mate.

Doc shrugged. "Some do."

"Does Ron know about shifters because that's really what I want to know." Especially after last night. It took all I had to not mark him right then and there. But that wouldn't be fair to him. He needed to pick me too, and humans didn't go by instincts. They needed more of a mark. I could only imagine Ron having a conversation with his buddy. "Oh, hey, I met this guy, and like, he's my forever." That was not at all how humans worked. Sure, they were into hot one-night stands, but that was a far cry from forever...and I couldn't just ask to have all his babies and watch them run around until they sprouted their fur. Actually, in a human/shifter mating, would they even sprout fur? I didn't know.

"As far as I know, he has no idea. Most of the town doesn't. But there are a few people here and there who are keeping our secrets."

"And other shifters?"

"There are a few of us. You already met me and Jase. Xander is a bunny, but from what I can tell, not the recessive-gene type of bunny. Are you a recessive gene cat or are you from a family of cats?"

I grimaced, hating to admit my inadequacy. "Lion defect."

"Not defect. You're a cat with a fierce lineage. Own it."

Own it. That was what I thought I had been trying to do by leaving, but all I'd really been doing was hiding. Maybe things could be different here.

"Is there like a clan or pack here? Am I stepping on any toes?" Or maybe I was welcome. How beautiful that would be...

"No pack. Although, as the numbers grow, it's looking like we might consider forming one at some point. For now, we're just happy to be living in the middle of nowhere and not dealing with all the hierarchal bull-shit that packs tend to foster."

How true that was. At least for lions.

We spent the next hour talking about all things related to shifters in town. I'd never lived in a place where shifters of different species all got along. And while I doubted that was strictly true, they were at peace.

"He almost marked me," I blurted out as Doc's phone alarm went off. He was hard core on that pie.

Doc didn't even look my way as he snoozed the alarm. "Because he's your mate."

Yeah, as if it was that simple. "Humans don't do that."

He got up and went to the door.

I followed behind, not wanting to be the reason he was late for that pie.

"He's your mate, and who knows...he may be a descendant of shifters."

"Then he might be my fated."

"Fate doesn't care about your descendants. That's not how it works. If he's your mate...he's your mate. All the rest is noise."

If that were the only noise, I'd be golden.

As it was, I had a house that was falling down, a sheriff trying to frame me for I didn't even know what, and no idea how I was going to deal with any of it.

"This might be the best thing I ever put in my mouth." Leo made yummy sounds around his fork.

"Agreed." I was lying. It was the second-best thing, but Doc didn't need to hear that. I'd already shared far more than I'd planned to with him.

"I still can't believe you've never had sugar pie." I had been waiting there with our pies already ordered when they arrived, including a second piece for Doc as Camille suggested.

He didn't turn it down. Good thing I did too, since they sold out five seconds after I walked through the door.

Leo's eyes rolled back in his head. "I want to make it

part of my life. Please tell me she makes it the same day every week so I can put it in my calendar."

I loved seeing his face light up like that. If it made him this giddy, he needed it more often, especially with the way things were going with his new home.

He was about to put another bite in his mouth when he stopped, holding the fork just an inch from his delicious lips. "Or is it one of those things you just have to know about?"

"You just have to be in the know." Doc started to work on his second piece. I was glad Camille had made the right call.

"I'm gonna need to get myself in the know."

While we ate our pies, we talked about benign things like the weather. Doc finished his quickly then excused himself to go pick up Xander from school. I was curious as to how he was going to handle the notes, but that wasn't any of my business. It was between the man and his son.

But still, I was a nosy Nelly and had a feeling it could go either one of two ways. One, they were notes from the mother to her son, just telling him all the things she wanted him to know before she passed. That would be heartbreaking and heart-wrenching and horrible in its own right, but at the same time, it would give some closure to a boy who lost too much too soon.

The second option, however, could be that she was letting him know things about his past. And since he had shifter blood, and we didn't know if she was a shifter, that could lead to more questions than answers.

"The sheriff hasn't called to say I could go back yet." Leo set down his fork, eyeing the last bit on my plate.

I pushed it his way. You only have one first time with sugar pie.

"I'm not surprised. He'll probably dawdle on that, if I'm being honest." Because he's an asshole. "What do you think about us heading into the city? Not the big city, but about a half hour from here. We can check out the home store."

He forked the last bit of my pie. "Yeah, that's a good idea. We can look around and place an order for delivery or organize everything to place an order since we don't know when I'll be able to get in."

He was going to need delivery for sure. Either that or a rental truck. Even with my truck, he'd be making multiple trips with the amount of supplies that place needed.

"That sounds like fun."

I smiled in agreement. Anything with him sounded fun.

"I've been meaning to do some things around the house for Mrs. Parker anyway." She mentioned the back fence was getting ratty. I figured I could fix that up for her so she didn't have to call someone in.

"You're like the ideal tenant."

"I try to be. There aren't that many places like it in town. They're usually either larger and perfect for families or just rented rooms." I took out a few bills to leave on the table to cover the pie.

Leo eyed the money on the table. "If you drive, I'll buy dinner."

"Deal." There was no point arguing about it. I wasn't that kind of alpha. Sure, I wanted to treat him, but if this was what he wanted, that's what he would get.

The trip to the home store turned out to be a blast. Starting over from the ground up meant we got to look at everything. There were a lot of choices to be made, and since we were only window shopping, they were stress-free.

We looked at bathroom fixtures and kitchen counter-tops and cabinets. I had to admit, I was impressed by how much a city boy knew about construction and finish work. I could do bare minimum repairs like fixing the fence or replacing a broken outlet. He, on the other hand, contemplated buying the tools to make his own cabinets.

By the time he was done, he came out with an entire notebook full of things he needed, complete with the order numbers and their prices. Ordering online at a later time was going to be a breeze. He wanted to order it all today, but not knowing when he could start work put a damper on that.

I had to work the next day so at least I could try to expedite things for him. He shouldn't be blocked from his own home. That was bullshit.

We stopped and ate dinner at a fancy steakhouse. It was his choice not mine. And it was perfect. Granted, we didn't fit in at all. Both of us were in our jeans and t-shirts, surrounded by suits and ties. All eyes were on my date, but not because of his clothes. He had a way of lighting up the room. Maybe it was the sparkle in his eyes. Maybe it was that smile he gave, the one that sucked you in. All I knew was it wasn't just me who was drawn in by him.

The entire way home, I wanted to ask him for more. More than just the night we had. The one we were both ignoring like a boss. And every time I was about to say something, I chickened out, not wanting to make things weird for him while he was still at my house.

But then his hand settled on my thigh and slowly started moving up. So freaking slowly. I almost questioned if it was moving at all. It was nice. Beyond nice. Maybe we didn't need the words. Maybe this was enough.

As we drove home in silence, just being together, only connected by that one hand, an unfamiliar peace settled over me.

I didn't want it to end.

"I have to confess something," Ron said as he shut the door behind us.

We'd had such an amazing time between the home store and dinner. And the way he'd brush against me as if it were the most natural thing in the world, I wasn't even sure he noticed he was doing it. He sure noticed when my hand climbed up his thigh. I wanted to beg him to pull over right there.

It wasn't easy, but I was good. I waited. Now, the waiting was over. "Oh, yeah? What's that?"

"When I said that pie was the best thing I ever put in my mouth."

He licked his bottom lip and then pulled it in with his teeth. He knew exactly where this was going. "Yeah."

"That was a lie."

"Oh really?" A shiver of desire ran up my spine.

Ron closed the distance between us. His body was so close to mine, yet not close enough. "Really."

I bit my lip, playing coy. "You didn't enjoy it?"

"Oh, I enjoyed it very much." He reached forward, grabbing my belt hoops with his forefingers. "But there is something I enjoy more."

"Me too," I whispered.

Ron didn't wait for more. He walked me straight to the bed, neither of us wanting to waste any time getting naked.

"I want you in my mouth," I said as I pulled his shirt over his head and tossed it on the ground.

He grinned. "But what if I want you in my mouth first?" He shoved his jeans past his hips until they puddled on the ground and he stepped out of them.

"Maybe we can do this together?" I shoved off my jeans as well and gave Ron a gentle shove onto the bed.

His beautifully naked body fell back with a soft bounce, and he stared up at me, his hard dick pointing straight up. The tip had a tiny bubble of moisture, and my mouth immediately started to water.

I climbed onto the bed beside him then threw my knee over his shoulder with a twist so he was staring up at my ass and his cock was just inches from my mouth.

Ron didn't give me a chance to get started before he pulled my hips down toward his face and sucked my balls into his mouth.

"Ungggh." My whole body felt a shock of pleasure as he sucked and teased me with his lips and tongue. I could have stayed in that position forever, but I had needs too, you know. I leaned forward and pulled his shaft into my mouth, sucking it down to the root as his head filled my throat. I held there as long as I could, loving the way he stretched me out before I had to pull back to let some air travel through to my lungs.

Ron's hips tilted up, chasing my mouth until I slid back down again. I loved that he wanted me so badly. Almost as badly as I wanted him.

We continued to stroke and tease and nip at each other until we couldn't hold back any longer. I wanted to feel him inside me, but I also wanted him exactly like this.

And more than anything, I wanted to come when he came. Feeling every inch of his body beneath mine as he gave it all to me, at the same time I gave it all to him. His finger snaked up my crack and then down to my hole, pressing against my opening.

I knew what was coming next, and I was desperate for it.

My hips instinctively tilted so he had better access, and as a result, the increased pressure of my cock at the sharp angle sent a spike of adrenaline through me. I moaned around him and squeezed his thighs as I got closer to release.

Ron's hips moved faster, pumping up into me at a frenzied pace as I pumped into him.

Just moments later, I felt it. The intense sensation pulling at my balls before exploding out of me, straight into his mouth.

As soon as the first load hit his tongue, he shoved his fingers deeper inside me, finding that spot within me that made everything so much better.

I did the same, slipping my fingers inside him as an orgasm rocked through his body and mine, moving us in sync as we both leaned into the pleasure of being with each other.

I was completely boneless as I lay upon him, wanting this moment to last forever but also wanting more.

I wasn't the only one with that idea. A few minutes later, Ron shifted our weight so we were side-by-side, still head to toe, and his tongue periodically darted out to lick my softening cock. "Now that was the best thing I've ever tasted."

My cat purred as I nestled my cheek against his leg, just wanting to be close to him. "I don't think anything could ever beat it. Will you stay with me tonight?"

Ron opened his mouth to speak but his phone pinged in his jeans. "Hold that thought."

The worst part about being with a cop is that he couldn't just ignore his phone when it rang. He was perpetually on-call. I listened with bated breath to find out what his answer would be. If he could stay, I knew he would. But when Ron sighed heavily and threw his head back in frustration, I knew it wasn't gonna happen.

"Yeah, I'm on my way." He disconnected the call and slowly turned to me. "I'm so sorry, but I have to go."

I nodded. "I know." I wanted to tell him it was okay, but it wasn't. I didn't blame him for leaving but I wanted more than anything to be in his arms until morning. "I'll see you tomorrow."

SIXTEEN
RON

The sheriff was getting ridiculous. Not getting. He *was* ridiculous. I really needed to figure out how to deal with him without making things worse for Leo. There was no reason why Leo shouldn't go back to his home. Although, truth be told, I didn't actually want him to leave my place.

I liked having him under my roof and in my bed, even if it wasn't the one I was in.

But that land was his home even before he fixed it up. He deserved to be there. He deserved to be allowed to rehab it, making it exactly the way he wanted.

By the time I got to the office after dealing with the overturned truck on the highway, it was pretty late.

The sheriff was gone for the day, and Ms. Patty had the night off. Since I had some privacy, I decided to dig a little further into the mess that was Clarence. That man continued to be a pain in my ass even after his death.

I looked through the files I could find, but I couldn't connect anything that made any sense. Other than a couple guns that Clarence shouldn't have had in his possession, there wasn't anything to worry about. Not from what I could tell. No weird threats or connections to groups that made threats. Nothing like that at all. He had just gone off the deep end and part of that included creating a mini arsenal.

Had the sheriff not been so sketch about it all, and those guns not been from our evidence, I'd have thought it was open and shut. It wasn't like the dead posed any danger. Maybe the serial numbers I pulled had been incorrect. But how was that possible? I was officially grasping at straws. But my gut said something bad was going on.

I just needed proof before I went any further. Starting something I couldn't finish would put me on the path to homelessness. Unlike the sheriff, I was an employee.

I could be gone just like that. And then the corruption, if there even was any, would only continue.

"Hello. Anybody here today?" Ms. Patty walked in and turned on lights in her path.

So much for her night off. "Yeah, I'm here. Hey." Great. I sounded like I was a guilty kid caught with their hand in the candy jar. I mean, technically, I was guilty of snooping but that wasn't really a crime. "So, tonight....you're working?" I wasn't making things better.

She slipped off her sweater. "Yeah, I need tomorrow off, so I figured I'd come in today and skip tomorrow."

"I'm pretty sure that isn't how scheduling works." I was only half teasing. Given the way Sheriff Martin had been lately, I'd be trying to avoid him too. If that was what she was doing.

She handled his bullshit far better than I did. It was pretty impressive.

"I wanted to talk to you about the sheriff." I felt compelled to ask about his behavior toward her, as uncomfortable as it was. Just because she was outwardly handling him like a boss didn't mean inwardly it wasn't getting to her.

"Thank goodness. Me too."

Okay, maybe she wasn't handling it as well as I thought. Every time I'd seen him get close to crossing the line again, she had squashed him like a bug, but maybe I missed something. Any trepidation I had for bringing it up fell away. "I noticed he's not always as professional with you as he should be."

"The man asked me out decades ago, and I told him I wished I could but I was already dating Hector, my husband. He believed that was the only reason and thinks he's hot stuff." She rolled her eyes and waved off my concern. "Ignore it. I do."

I sighed. "It's not okay. He's your boss."

"Don't you worry about me. We have bigger fish to fry." She looked around the room, then lowered her voice. "Last Friday was a slow day, and I didn't have much to do up front here. I thought to myself, hey, that back room looks like a toddler was set free in it, maybe I should clean it up and organize it a bit."

She started to walk away from me, and then she turned and gave me her teacher look, the one that said you better keep up. So I did.

"See here?" She pointed to the room. "It's a mess, right?"

"Definitely." I waited for Ms. Patty to sing the clean-up song or whatever she used to do in her classroom.

"But it's worse than that. Alright, I'm just gonna say it. Not everything's where it's supposed to be and I think things are missing."

"What are you saying?" The two guns that came up as being here but were most definitely from Clarence's had my brain already working.

"I think he takes things."

I was grateful she assumed the thief was him and not me. "Not me?"

"You're not that type, and even if I thought you were, some of these date back to before you arrived." How many hours did she spend in here? "Like, there was a necklace that somebody found down by the river. It was really nice. So nice, there was a picture of it in the paper, and I gave my husband guff for not buying me jewelry anymore."

I could totally see her doing that. Especially now that I'd seen her in action. "And it's not there anymore?"

"Nope, and there's no claim ticket anywhere. According to the documents, it's still here. But here's the weirdest part. I saw it on eBay."

I tried to piece together the time frame. "It was missing years ago."

"No, it was logged in here years ago, and before you ask how I know it was the same one, it had an inscription that matched. And yes, I did a reverse photo search so quit giving me the eye."

I chuckled. "Don't tell me you bought it." Or maybe she should've to see if it matched?

"No, don't be ridiculous. Of course I didn't buy it. If I bought it, he would know it was me and it would miraculously disappear." She tsked.

"So what did you do?" Because she did something or she wouldn't be here acting like Angela in that murder mystery show. "I had my cousin buy it."

"Did she get it?"

"Uh huh. And it's the same one, I know it. And guess where the PO box it came from was?"

I shrugged.

"Bakersville." Only one town over.

"It could be a coincidence." My gut said it wasn't.

"I know, but there are a lot of other things missing too, and I haven't even gotten very far with the organization. Every time I think I have time to dig deeper, he comes back."

I raised an eyebrow. "You're not here so you can have tomorrow off, are you?"

"Well, I'm taking the day off, but no. I thought today I could go finish in the room and maybe you could help me look into the sheriff's shenanigans. I can tell by your color green that this is making you as nauseous as it's been making me. Don't get me wrong. I never liked the guy, but I've seen him change over the years."

"Is that why you took this job?" Today was not turning out the way I expected, but in a way, it was. I wanted to see what the sheriff was up to, and it was being handed to me on a platter.

"No. I took this job because I wanted to open my school back up and my husband said it sucked up too much of my time—which it did. Then this job opened up, so I figured why not? Decent pay, minimal hours, close to home. I didn't expect to stumble upon a huge crime caper."

"You realize this could go very badly." Arresting a sheriff wasn't impossible, but there was a reason you didn't hear about it often.

"So, you're not telling me no?" She clapped her hands together.

Here I was wanting to puke and she looked like she was about to go to an amusement park wearing mouse ears.

"No, I'm not telling me no." I chuckled then broke down and told her everything I knew. We spent the next five hours cross-referencing everything catego-rized as evidence and all the things that remained unclaimed.

In a way, what we found was a relief. The sheriff wasn't arming random crazies. He was selling things to make money. It was crappy and wrong, but knowing where the only two missing guns went was a relief.

By the end of the night, we had enough information to at least get a search warrant and most likely a conviction. All we needed to do was tie the PO box to his PayPal, and that would be pretty easy with the warrant. The question was what were we going to do about it. Once the warrant was issued...things would explode in town. We had to tread lightly.

Ms. Patty arched her back to stretch it out and then looked at me. "Sit on it, Ron. Trust me."

I stared at the lists in front of me. "I'm not sure I can do that."

"I grew up in small-town politics, and while you have been here long...just trust me. Give me three days."

I didn't like that idea. Not. One. Bit. But I didn't know where to start so a few days felt reasonable.

"Get that look off your face. I won't do anything that will get either of us in trouble."

"Why don't I believe that?"

The phone started ringing, and unlike my cell, we couldn't let it just ring. "Just don't do anything. Let me think on this."

I ran to answer the phone and then went out to the river where someone was sure there was a rabid skunk, which turned out to be a rock because the lady was mostly blind.

By the time I got back to the office, Ms. Patty was gone.

It didn't go unnoticed that she never agreed not to do anything with her knowledge.

My life just kept getting more complicated.

SEVENTEEN

LEO

"GOOD NEWS!" RON WAS SCRAMBLING SOME EGGS. He'd taken to making me breakfast, which I had to admit, I really liked.

I'd been making more of the dinners. Although making was a very loose definition of the word. Half the time, we went to the diner. I was okay with that. There were far worse ways to spend the evening than working my way through the menu and getting to know the regulars while spending time with Ron.

Between the two of us, we really couldn't cook worth a damn. Ron had breakfast down pat and could boil spaghetti like nobody's business. And I could make a mean sandwich and yummy popcorn, so we weren't completely inept.

The two of us were eating quite nicely, thank you very much.

I tried not to think of us as the two of *us*. I was just a houseguest to him. A houseguest with benefits, but still...we hadn't agreed to anything more. Sure, he was my mate and I chose him, but that didn't mean it went both ways. Humans were...different.

The entire thing was just so confusing.

"Morning. Why did you get out of bed so early?" I wanted to cuddle. It was a side effect of being a cat. I loved that we were now sharing a bed each night. I didn't even pretend to go to my own.

"Long story short, or short story long?" he asked, dishing up a plate of eggs.

"I'll go with long story short, and some coffee. Lots of coffee." I was exhausted for some reason, and I needed to shake it off.

"We need to head to the station." He handed me a plate of eggs, bacon, and toast.

"Maybe I should've asked for the long version." I sat at the counter and waited for him to join me.

He sat down beside me with his own plate.

"Thanks." I kissed his cheek. "I'm starving, and this is perfect. So, the long version?"

"I got a text from Mayor Edison asking me to meet him at the station." I'd met the mayor at the diner. Nice enough guy—a possum from what I could gather. It wasn't exactly diner conversation, but he was a shifter for sure.

"Oh, so you have to go, and I can stay home and be lazy." Worked for me. I was ready for a nap. I'd been working from Ron's house while he worked, keeping my vacation time open for when we could go back to work on the house. Today, though...I was too tired to do anything.

"And then..." He pointed to my plate with his fork and waited for me to grab a piece of the toast. "Remember, it's the long version..." He cocked an eyebrow. "The sheriff called and told me to be at the station at nine with you."

I looked at the clock on the microwave. Eight fifteen. Great.

"Says he has some questions for you."

Fuck. I knew this was coming. Ron had been edgy about anything related to work, so I had a feeling he expected it too. That didn't make it suck less. "So, a good time will be had by all," I teased, the dread building in my belly.

"Something like that."

We finished our breakfast and got to the station just on time.

"Thought you would be a no-show," the sheriff barked as we walked in. Such a pleasant man...ugh.

"Ron said you needed to speak with me?" No sense making this harder than it already was.

"Ron, is it? Not Deputy Ron?" What an ass.

"Deputy Ron."

"'Bout time you showed some respect. Ron, you're dismissed. Leo, if that even is your real name, you sit here."

"I have some work to do, so I appreciate that." Ron smirked as he went to sit at his desk. Where was the popcorn?

I sat where the sheriff said to, watching Ron the entire time.

"I said you were dismissed. You can leave now." Please don't leave.

"Actually I can't. I promised the mayor I would meet him here in fifteen minutes."

"Fine." He huffed off to his chair and sat down, scowling at me the entire time.

"I need to fingerprint you and run the prints."

What? "Why?"

"Because you're the owner of record of the property with the stolen guns." Stolen? When did that happen?

Ron piped in, my knight in shining armor. "What was stolen, exactly?"

"Two of the guns were stolen from evidence." What?

I looked to Ron who seemed less concerned about it than I expected. I was being accused of stealing guns—guns from a police station as if I could manage that if I wanted to.

"Are you saying you won't cooperate?"

The door opened. Thank goodness. I needed to figure out what was happening. It had to be more than face value or Ron wouldn't be so nonchalant. Come to think of it, he wasn't that upset when he told me about coming down here.

"Mayor, nice to see you again." I gave a half wave. "I'm just here getting fingerprinted for stealing guns from the department and then sealing them up in a secret room of a house I bought a few weeks ago from a dead man with a criminal past."

Ms. Patty walked in and stood behind him. "Oh, honey, you couldn't have done that. Don't be silly."

"He is the owner of record," the sheriff reiterated as if saying it enough made the words hold value.

"Sheriff, I'm here today to show you something." He held his hand out and a third person stepped in the door, someone I didn't know, another shifter by the scent of him, and handed him a folder.

"Mayor, the town meeting is next week." The vein in the sheriff's neck throbbed as his breath quickened.

"I can read it for you if you want, boss." Ms. Patty was looking extremely pleased with herself. She grabbed the folder like she was in charge and opened it up. "Oh my...look at this. You have the same name and permanent address as an eBay seller with a PO box just one town over from here."

"Would that be the same seller who sold that gorgeous necklace, the one with the same inscription as the one that was featured in the paper many moons ago?" Ron sidled up to me, taking my hand and letting me know it was time to get up.

"Martin is hardly an uncommon name." His inflection made me think I shouldn't be right in front of him. He was about to explode.

Ron must've heard it too, scooting us to the side as the third person started to ramble on about codes from the town statutes.

I couldn't even focus on what he was saying as my mate continued to separate me from the threat.

The sheriff came around his desk, his hand too close to his holster for my liking. "You can't do this."

"Let me see that. There must be a mistake." Ron stepped away from me. What was he doing? "There's no way Sheriff Martin would be mixed up in anything illegal." He most certainly did know he would.

Mate. Protect. He was protecting me. Please don't let me need protecting.

"I think it's time you all left." The sheriff was crazy if he thought all three of them would just leave after they showed up with a pile of evidence that I didn't quite understand. Then again, I didn't need to. I just needed to be out of the way. Why the fuck wasn't Ron out of the way?

"Funny..." Ms. Patty tapped the folder in her hand. "We were thinking the same thing.'

"This town doesn't need a huge media splash." Mayor Edison spoke slowly as if he were on half speed. "If only there were a way to get you gone so this wasn't a concern for us any longer."

"According to the town codes, the sheriff is permitted to resign mid-term if he's moving from the state," the man I didn't know piped in.

"Are you saying..." The sheriff reached for his holster, and Ron was right there to intercept him.

"Let me help you there." Ron reached for the gun and held his hand out for the badge.

The sheriff seemed too stunned to know how to respond. "And if I do..."

"Then all of this goes away. No one needs the trouble." Mayor Edison took the folder back from Ms. Patty.

Sheriff Martin had his resignation in and his house on the market an hour later. The man I didn't know, the one with the codes and statutes, happened to be the owner of the real estate agency in town. As it turned out, that was no coincidence.

"How much did you know about all that?" I asked Ron when we were finally alone.

"Most of it," he confessed. "The only unknown was you being there. That had been a surprise. I didn't like it."

"I didn't either." I wrapped my arms around him. "When you got close to him... Well, let's avoid that again, okay?"

"Were you jealous?" He kissed the top of my head at the same time that I smacked his chest playfully.

"More like, I didn't want you shot."

He dropped his jaw, feigning shock. "You like having me around?"

"Who else is going to bring me to sugar pie day?" I leaned up, kissed his lips too chastely for my liking, and brought them around to his ear, whispering, "Today is sugar pie day."

"I love it when you sweet talk me, omega mine."

Omega Mine. The only two words sweeter than sugar pie.

EIGHTEEN
RON

"I can go home now," Leo said out of nowhere. We were chatting about the music of all things.

"You can stay here." I took his hand in mine. "I'd like you to stay here."

"I'd like to stay here."

When he agreed to stay with me, my heart was exactly where I wanted it to be. It was too soon by anybody's standards. You didn't randomly meet a guy, bring them home, get it on, and then just keep him. Not even if it was under the guise of giving him shelter. You just didn't do that. But that was exactly what I did, and it was the best decision of my life.

He had no excuse to stay. Technically, he didn't need to be here anymore. Living in a camper beside a dilapidated shack was not what I called ideal housing for anyone, but he would no longer get fines and his camper impounded if he chose it.

Not that the shack would be one for long. We left the diner and went straight to the home store, ordering everything under the sun. On Monday morning, it would all be delivered, and then the hard work would begin.

Monday would also be my first day as interim sheriff. What a wild and crazy day.

"YOU ARE SO TALENTED." I walked into the house to find the cabinets already in place. "They're stunning." The fact that he could take wood and turn it into cabinets blew my mind.

"They're a bitch to hang." Jase came in from the back entrance. "Good thing they'll last a lifetime."

"Good thing he has a strong friend who can help." The guilt of working so many hours was real. The town voted to look for a new deputy sheriff, but I was fine with that being a slow process. The last thing I needed was to be out of a job come election day. Ms. Patty swore it would be an easy win. But man, votes to keep your job—not really my thing.

"He just needed some dumb muscle." Jase chuckled. "And this dumb muscle needs to head home. Date night." He winked.

Seeing how in love he and August were was nice. I could see myself with Leo like that. The more time I spent with him, the more I liked him...loved him. That scary four-letter word wasn't so scary now that I understood what it meant.

It meant that he was the first thing I thought about in the morning and the last before I went to sleep and a thousand other times throughout the day. I missed him, and even if we did nothing but occupy the same space together, I felt more at home there than anywhere I'd ever been. My every decision had a component of *What About Leo* in it, right down to what to pick up for dinner. I had it bad, and I wouldn't have it any other way.

I had it so bad that I was ready to put a ring on it. I just needed to figure out the best way to give it to him.

Jase left so I took a good look around the home. The walls were up, the floors laid, and now the kitchen cabinets were done. There was still more work to do, but it would be done soon—sooner than I wanted. Which made me a prick, but I couldn't help it. I wanted him in my bed every night, not just on date night.

"I missed you." Leo walked into my open arms. "Today was tough."

I'd never hung cabinets, but the sheer fact they were still on the wall had me impressed. I'd had small photos fall off mine.

"I missed you too. I'm glad Jase was here to help." He was one of a group of helpers who randomly showed up, claiming they were bored. They weren't bored. It was the town's way of saying he was both accepted and wanted.

He'd still be the new guy for many years, but he was their new guy.

Leo froze in my arms, then pushed away and bolted to the bathroom.

Not again. He'd been sick quite a few times lately. At first, he said it was too much coffee, so he stopped drinking it. Then he thought it was from eating crappy food like a bag of chips for lunch while he worked, so I started making him lunches. Yesterday, I was starting to wonder if it was something more serious, and I casually mentioned it to Ms. Patty.

At lunch, I found a box with two pregnancy tests on my desk. They were now in my glove box—with the wedding ring I bought last week. I didn't know how to do things in order. Move in first, date second, get pregnant third—pregnant. Holy shit. I was going to be a dad.

"Sorry. I thought I was better." He came out, his face still damp from when he splashed water over it.

I took him by the hand and brought him out to the truck.

He was confused when I opened up the glove box and showed him the pregnancy tests.

"You think I'm pregnant?" he asked, taking one out and looking at it like it was some kind of alien artifact.

I looked him straight in the eye. "You've been sick."

"Lots of people get sick."

"Yeah, I know. But I just...I feel like you might be, so amuse me?" What was the worst that could happen?

He could leave me.

His hand immediately went to his belly. "And if I am?"

"Well, if you are, then you're gonna have a baby." Our baby.

"We're gonna have a baby." He looked up at me, still clutching the test in one hand and holding his belly with the other.

"Yeah, I think maybe we are." I kissed his cheek. "Let's go find out."

"But seriously, what if I am?" he asked again.

I pulled him closer into my side. "Then we're going to be fathers."

"I'm scared." He took a step toward the house and stopped. "Really scared."

I kissed his temple. "Good thing I'll be by your side."

"Even if?"

"Even if."

NINETEEN
LEO

Two days ago, I heard a faint echo and my stupid cat kept saying, *Kit. Kit. Kit.*

I ignored him.

Apparently, I was quite good at that, blocking out what my cat was trying to say. Being too frightened to even listen.

It was getting harder, though, because with each day, he was getting more and more demanding. First it was *mate, mate, mate,* then it was *kit, kit, kit,* and now he was rattling on with *claim, claim, claim.* He didn't understand the difference between humans and shifters. He only understood that fate put Ron there for us.

He was smarter than me.

Yesterday, the echo became undeniably a heartbeat, or possibly more than one heartbeat.

Still, I ignored it. I didn't dare dream it could be true. And if it were true, what it would look like. So, instead, I lived in the happy little land of denial. Until Ron showed up all sweet, tests awaiting, and it was the moment of truth.

I went into the bathroom, tore open the boxes and took both tests. If one answer was good—two were better.

And with each second that went by, my panic started to increase. But it wasn't because I might be having a baby. I did already love the little guy or guys or gals or whatever. No, I was scared to think that I might not be pregnant. And there was the possibility that if I was pregnant, Ron might not be okay with it.

For shifters and their mates, the joy of pregnancy kind of went along with their bond, but it was different with humans. I'd heard too many stories of deadbeat dads and dads who left and baby daddies. I was terrified. The rational side of me told me I shouldn't be, because Ron wasn't like that. And he never acted like he was for even a second. It was just my own insecurities attacking me from the inside.

We went inside to the newly finished bathroom of our mostly finished house, because it was ours...maybe not according to the title or even with our spoken words, but we both built it out of nothing. And, at the end of the day, I wouldn't have it at all if it weren't for Ron. He and Ms. Patty. I still didn't understand all that went down, but it had shifter written all over it. The only human there had been Ms. Patty, and she was mated to a wolf based on the scar I caught a glimpse of as she left.

"So, what does it say?" Ron was pacing outside the bathroom door when I came out.

"It says to wait three minutes." Which sounded like an eternity.

"Three minutes left or from when you went in?" He was as anxious to find out as I was and started to head in.

"No, don't watch the sticks." I placed my hand on his arm, needing the contact more than trying to prevent him from entering. "No looking before it's time. I don't want to get false hopes, or have my heart shattered a moment before I have to."

He turned around and hugged me tight. "But if I keep pestering you about it, then the three minutes that are left will be down to two. And then one and then we can look."

"That's one way to look at it, I guess." I held on to him tightly, neither of us speaking, as I counted our breaths.

"Are we going to look now?" he asked less than a minute later.

"Fine, but if we look now and it doesn't show a second line, we wait it out."

"Deal," he agreed and took my hand.

My logic was that the double line would show, but it wouldn't unshow and give us a false positive—that and I needed to look.

We walked in, hand in hand, and each picked up a stick, holding it out so we could both see. I looked at the one in my hand—two lines. I looked at the one in his hand—two lines.

"We're gonna be dads," we both said at the same time.

"Are you still gonna stay with me?" I asked, my hand trembling slightly.

"I was thinking more that we could live in the house you built for our family."

"Our family." He put his stick down and placed his hand on my belly. "Our family. I love you, Leo." He kissed me hard and fast. A little too fast for my liking.

But that didn't matter because he loved me. He might not have an inner animal telling him I was his mate, but his heart did, and in a way, that made it more special.

"And I love you." I threw my arms around him, kissing him deeply, needing to taste him, touch him, feel his knot.

And then the sharp corner of the countertop jabbed into my side and I flinched.

"Maybe we best take this to another room?" Not that there was a lick of furnishings anywhere, but we could make do. At least it wouldn't mark me in the non-fun way.

"I guess the guest bathroom wasn't the best place to start." He kissed me on the cheek and led me out of the bathroom.

"So, is that a yes, will you live with me?" It wasn't enough, but it was a start. We could build our way up to me explaining that his boyfriend sprouts fur and purrs.

"That depends. Will you marry me?"

"You don't have to because I'm—" He cut me off with a finger to my lips.

"No, no, no—believe me, it's not that. You'll see." He led me out to his truck, this time opening the compartment between the seats. He reached in and pulled out a little blue box. He set it in my hand and then took out his wallet and pulled out a receipt. "See this date? It's from before you were even sick once. This is not because of our baby. I love you. I was...scared to move too fast...to scare you away."

I opened the box and there it was, a set of rings—rings that to humans meant forever. He wanted me forever.

TWENTY

RON

I was on top of the world. I had a man I loved, who by some miracle loved me back, a baby on the way, our home was ready for us to move in, and I was the sheriff, at least for now. I still wasn't sure how Ms. Patty managed to pull all that together. And as much as I wanted justice done, I knew this was the best thing for the town. Martin was greedy and that greed led him to some shitastic choices, but it felt like a crime of opportunity and having him scared and gone was the right thing to do. I hoped.

"Ms. Patty, I'm going to head out a bit early today. I want to surprise Leo." His poor cat had been with Jase and August for way too long. The house was ready enough for him to be there, and I had a delivery of pet supplies sitting in my truck. I was bringing his fur baby home.

I pulled into their driveway with Henrietta making it known I was there.

"Sheriff!" August came around to the side of the house. "What brings you here?"

"It's time to bring Leo's cat home." I grabbed the cat carrier off the back of my truck, and August went pale.

"What? Did something happen to him?"

"No. Of course not." Jase came up behind August. "I'll go get him. Why don't you put some tea on and I'll be right back. Angeline was sound asleep when I just checked on her, but maybe she will wake up and get some Uncle Ron time by the time tea is over."

"Yeah, sorry," August mumbled. "My stomach is off— I'm not sick, it's just...I ate tacos."

Okay then. Tacos made my tummy happy but... "Are you...you know?" I asked.

He grinned. "I hope so."

"I hope so too."

We went inside and he put on the kettle as I got out the cookies. I loved how traditions of Angeline's were still so vibrant in the house.

Lux jumped up onto the chair beside me. "How are you, gorgeous? Did you have fun with Lion? He must miss his daddy." I still felt awful about Leo needing to be away from his cat, which was why I decided to surprise him.

Only he surprised me instead, walking into the kitchen and kissing me on the cheek, flashing his ring to August.

August squeed. "Show me the ring!"

Jase mumbled something that sounded remarkably like, "Human" as he came in empty-handed.

August was inspecting the cut like a professional jeweler. "It's perfect."

"Where's the cat?" I asked. He was the reason I was here, and yet I'd not seen whiskers nor tail of him.

"Yeah, about that." August walked around the counter to turn off the now-whistling kettle.

"Did something happen?" I'd never forgive myself if my offer was the reason something happened to Leo's cat. Never.

"Just have a seat while I get the tea. There's nothing to worry about." That didn't sound close to true, and the way Leo went green, it didn't sound good to him either.

"It'll be fine," Jase reassured Leo and held a seat out for him. "I promise. Don't you worry."

"What happened to the cat?" I sat as close to Leo as I could. This was bad. So very bad.

"Nothing happened to his cat. I promise." August set the tea in front of me and pushed the cookie tin my way. Like I could eat with this dread building up inside of me.

"There are some things that need explaining about your cat, and it's best to do when we're all together." August sat down.

"It's fine, Ron. Promise." Leo didn't sound fine.

"Remember that day we were at your place watching the game and you thought it was a good idea to see if they had sugar pie?" August asked Ron.

"Even though it was dinner time and would be long gone. Yeah, I remember. What does that have to do with this?" We had gone all the way there to have Camille ask us if we were joking, and when we said we weren't, she sent us on our way with apple pie which was good...but not the same.

"Remember the peacock?" Jase grabbed a cookie.

"Of course I do. They stick out here. It was a peahen, though...the tail is the giveaway." It was stunning and then it was gone and I accidentally...

"Why are you blushing?" Leo asked.

"I walked around to get a better look, and then I saw Ms. Patty, but she was...naked. Damn, I had done a good job forgetting about that. Why did you have to do that, asshat." I threw my napkin at Jase.

"No way!" Leo looked to Jase who nodded. "I didn't sense that at all."

"Birds are lucky like that." Jase shrugged.

"So the...oh...so much is making sense now." Leo and Jase were having some kind of a secret code meeting and there was still no cat.

"You guys are making things harder than they need to be." August took back control of the conversation. "Ron, it's story time. I'm going to tell you about the awesome that is Jase and me."

"I already know that tale...it ends in happily ever after with the most adorable little girl I've ever met." What I wanted to know about was the cat.

"The story gets more interesting. Once upon a time, I was here minding my own business, trying to figure out how to take care of my grandma's animals, when Xander came over with a rabbit. It was a cute little thing, but he was in bad shape—stupid fox thought he was dinner. My heart hurt for him." I remembered that. That rabbit was weird. Come to think of it, I hadn't seen him around lately either.

"No vet would come to help and they told me it would be kinder to put him down." He reached out for Jase's hand. "But I just couldn't do it." He kissed Jase's cheek and whispered in his ear.

Jase got up and walked to the open area of the kitchen.

Jace then took his shirt off and reached for his pants.

"Is this a naked storytime, because we're not, I mean...I'm not...are you...? I don't think this is our thing." I looked to Leo. He never once hinted about being poly or even a swinger or whatever Jase getting naked might indicate, but maybe? My head was spinning.

"No, it's definitely not not my thing." Leo gave August a look I couldn't decipher as Jase continued to remove his pants until he was standing buck-ass naked, his bits just hanging out.

"It wasn't until after he healed that I figured out this was no ordinary bunny." Was August still telling a story as his husband stood there in all his naked glory—not that I was looking. Except I was. I was like a deer caught in freaking headlights.

"This bunny was..."

And then Jase was gone. Just vanished. And in his place was...a bunny.

Holy shit.

Jase was an animal.

TWENTY-ONE
LEO

WHEN I GOT THE CALL FROM JASE, I RACED RIGHT over, my heart pounding so forcefully in my chest I could hardly breathe.

I had two choices. I could foster a lie and say something happened to my cat—keeping my mate in the dark until he was the father of kittens. Since, from what I could tell, there were at least three heartbeats. Or, I could face the music and let him know I was my cat and pray everything worked out as well for us as it did for Jase and August.

Both options were terrifying and could result in me losing everything.

And then I got there and Ron, dear sweet Ron, was so worried about Lion, and he could tell something was up—and that only compounded my guilt. I needed to just tell him. I knew I did. But I was frozen.

So instead, I listened to the story about Ms. Patty, whom Ron had unknowingly discovered was a bird— something I still was shocked by. I'd never not sensed a shifter before. Except now I was wondering if I had. Maybe Ron was the only human in town and the entire place was a bird colony.

And still I froze.

August understood, probably better than I did. He'd been *the human*. He got it. And when he took the lead, I let him.

"I'm not into sharing," I said, reaching around my mate's shoulders. "It's only you."

"Jase—rabbit—Jase—" he stammered.

"My mate is a shifter." August puffed out his chest as Jase shifted back, this time clearly aroused. Stupid bunnies and their shifting horniness.

"No one wants to see that." I shook my head.

"I want to see that," August sassed.

"You're a...a bunny?" Ron didn't move. That was a good sign, right? He could've run away and instead he was glued to his chair.

Or maybe he was in shock.

What a clusterfuck.

"I'm a shifter and my animal is a bunny and Lion is—"

"Leo's pet cat is a person? No. That's just...how could he do that to him? Isn't that like...whoa, like the rat in those books. Is he a spy?" Ron stood up, arms on my shoulders as he looked around the room. I could almost hear the wheels turning. He thought I was in danger.

"I'm pretty sure I couldn't fuck this up any more than I already have, so it's on you, Leo." August took a long sip of his tea.

Way to throw me under the bus.

I totally deserved it.

"Ron...I'm Lion, just like Jase is a bunny and..."

"Ms. Patty is a bird?" he finished for me.

"Yeah." I stood up, needing to be face to face with him, needing to be looking in his eyes.

"What else?"

"What are you asking?" I took a tiny step forward. When he didn't move, I reached out and put my hand on his chest.

"What else is a lie? Just the cat thing?"

Lie. I sucked. I had lied. Maybe I didn't say *I'm just a human, nothing weird here,* but omission is a lie. And I'd done it so easily, just as I'd been raised to. Humans were the threat of every story told. Ron wasn't a threat, though. My cat recognized it instantly.

If only I had listened.

"Umm, yeah, isn't that enough?" Because I had feared it would be a deal breaker.

"So you are *you* except for that?" His hand reached up and cupped my cheek. "The you that makes me smile in the morning as I watch you sleep, the you that can't cook but can get a mean carryout, the you who makes me laugh, the you that supported me when things were shit at work, the you who makes me want to come home, the you who is my home."

"I'm me." My voice cracked. His words were so sweet, his acceptance so complete.

He threw his arms around me. "And you love me." It wasn't a question.

I squeezed him back. "I do—so much." There was so much more to say on that...on all of this, but for now, that would be enough. I loved him. He loved me.

"And nothing else...right...no big surprises?" He squished his nose, his eyes doing that thing they did when he was teasing me...the little glint that had me...well, it had me in the same predicament Jase was in.

We needed to get out of here and give them some privacy and get us some of our own.

"None," I promised.

"Thank fuck." His lips crashed into mine, and he kissed me with so much passion it was a miracle I didn't melt into a pile of goo right then and there. The kiss only ended when Angeline started to coo over the baby monitor. I half heard one of the guys say something about getting her.

"I was so scared I was going to have to tell you your cat was dead."

"So you're not pissed or freaked out or whatever?" Because I would've been all those things and more. Sitting in the chair beside him, every horrible ending to me telling him had played out...every single one of them resulting in me being alone. I'd been fine being alone, but now that I knew what it was like to truly be complete...the thought was unbearable.

"I mean, I have questions...lots and lots of questions, but you're still you—and I love you, so isn't that just details." God, I loved him.

We left the farm and went back to the home that was to be ours and talked about all things, and by the time the sun had set, everything finally felt right in my world.

Mate.

Except maybe for my pestering cat.

TWENTY-TWO

RON

"I WAS THINKING ABOUT WHAT YOU SAID...A LOT." I came out of the bathroom, a towel around my waist, Leo on our bed, shirt off, his hands on his already-rounded belly. When he told me babies, not baby, and then Doc confirmed it, I'd been floored, but it didn't really sink in. Now that he was starting to show already, something Doc said would happen with this many babies, not that he said how many babies that was, it was starting to become real and I couldn't wait.

"I say a lot of things. Are you talking about the hand-cuffs? Because that was a joke...unless you don't want it to be?" How did he think I was going to concentrate with him being all sexy like that?

He pulled the blanket off him, his erection now exposed. *He wanted me to concentrate on that.*

"The guys will be here in a couple hours," I reminded him. "We still need to finish packing the kitchen." Which I had officially deemed the worst job ever.

Today was the day we would officially move into our new home. Jase, Doc, and Edison were all going to bring their trucks and help us get the furniture moved and then we would be home. I loved that word.

It had been only a week since August told me about Leo being a shifter, and in that time, everything changed—or maybe not changed so much as started to make sense.

Leo was mine and I was his, and it was more than just dating or even the engagement. It was on a cellular level. When he told me about the mate thing, he confessed his fear that I wouldn't get it. Only thing was, I got it before then. He just put a name on it. He also made me feel less like a freak for wanting to bite him and leave a mark because that desire only got stronger with each knotting.

"I want to be mated when we move in," I blurted out. So much for my sexy seduction.

"Mating is forever." Leo climbed up off the bed.

"I guess if you can't promise me longer than that, I'll have to accept forever." I dropped my towel.

Leo slowly walked into my arms, an intense look of affection and excitement peering back at me through his beautiful eyes. "Well, then, what are you waiting for?" He dropped over my body, his chest against mine as our hard cocks were pressed together.

My mouth instantly went to his, kissing and licking him as my hands explored his body. I wanted to touch every inch of him, but I had to settle for his back and sides before sliding my fingers over his ass and pulling his cheeks apart.

Leo was ready for me, and so was his cat. His hips rocked as he waited for me to enter him, joining our bodies in a way that would never be undone.

My teeth closed around his lip and I pulled back, teasing him for what was about to happen.

Using my hands to reposition his hips and pelvis, I moved Leo's opening so it was right above my dick, but I didn't press in yet. My eyes locked on his and we stared at each other for a long moment. "Forever?"

He grinned and nodded his head. "Forever."

I pressed up as he pressed down, joining us in the way we both so desperately needed. I wanted this moment to last hours, days even. But neither of us were able to hold back the excitement of what we were doing.

After only a few moments of thrusting up into him while Leo slammed down onto me, we were both precariously close to release.

With my hand wrapped behind his neck, I gently pulled him forward and kissed him hard as I increased my pace inside his ass. When we were both ready, I dragged my lips across his cheek and down his neck until I could feel the pulsing of blood flowing beneath his skin.

As if our bodies were fully in sync with what we needed, my teeth closed down on his tender skin, breaking through the surface and marking him in a way that proved to the world he was mine forever.

"Ron!" Leo cried out just before his teeth dug into my shoulder, marking me in return, as we both came in slow, deep convulsions that rocked through us.

It was unlike any orgasm I'd ever experienced. Instead of a fleeting high with a trailing low, this felt like a lifetime of love and joy and passion and pleasure all pulled together to bring us this moment.

My forehead rested against Leo's as we both struggled to catch our breath. "I love you."

Leo tilted up just enough for his lips to brush against mine. "I love you too, alpha."

I WOKE UP, the both of us having dozed off in each other's arms, to a knock on the front door.

"Wake up, mate." I loved the sound of that. "They're here."

He sprang up so fast. "The kitchen."

"It'll get done." I kissed the spot where I bit him, oddly proud of the mangled skin, and climbed out of bed, grabbing a pair of jeans as the knock on the door got progressively louder.

"I'm coming," I called as I slid the jeans on and jogged to the door, opening it up to find all three men there.

"Oh, I see that's true." Edison brushed past me. "Is all of this being moved?"

"You guys are..." The best friends ever. Our relationships had changed, just in the week. It was as if knowing about them opened up a new level for us. Heck, Edison had been a *sometimes have pie with* kind of friend and now we talked...like, really talked when he stopped by to work on mayoral business. And with all the changes, was quite frequent.

It was nice.

"The best." Doc slapped the back of my shoulder. "We know. Now let's get you and your mate moved."

EPILOGUE

LEO

"Doc's back in town." Ron plopped on the couch beside me and wrapped his arm around me. "He called on my way home."

Doc had gone on a mysterious trip, and left Xander at the farm with Jase and August. I had a feeling it had something to do with what was inside the letters, but Doc only shared as much as he shared. At least that had been my experience.

"That means I can get these babies outta me." I was so done being pregnant. The little guys liked to kick like nobody's business.

"I kind of like you pregnant." Ron's hand rubbed small circles on my belly. He wasn't even being nice either.

And I thought he couldn't keep his hands off me before. He was a walking hard-on now, which totally worked for me given I was as well. I might not have been as flexible as I was before, but I was definitely on the willing train, at least until yesterday. I'd been feeling kind of weird since then. I was pretty sure the babies had dropped.

"Don't even," I teased as I pushed myself out of the couch. "I gotta walk."

I put my hands under my stomach, the strain of the weight starting to get to me. It hadn't been uncommon in my pride for an omega to have three or more babies, but now that I was in their position, carrying four, I saw how amazing that feat was.

"Feeling okay today?"

"Yeah. I think so. I just need to walk or maybe...can we go see Doc?" I hated to do that given he'd just come home, but I needed the reassurance that this off-kilter feeling was just normal pregnancy stuff.

"I'll call him." He took out his phone as I waddled over to the bathroom. Four babies on a bladder made me a frequent visitor.

Not that I would change anything. I was so excited to be a father. Work had allowed me to adjust my case-load as my pregnancy drew closer to the due date and they were willing to be flexible with me after the babies arrived. Ron had suggested multiple times that I quit altogether, and I was considering it. But having the job waiting if I needed it was nice.

"He said he's voting but can meet us in a bit."

I was officially the worst mate in the entire universe. "Grab your keys." I worked my way out the front door and to our van. Yes, we were those dads, complete with a minivan. It was amazing.

I got in the passenger side seat as he reached his door. "You just want to go to Doc's because you haven't seen him in a while, right? Nothing's wrong?" My poor alpha was worried. Yeah, I really was the worst mate ever.

"I need to vote. I spaced on what day it was." Which should've been impossible since I'd been the one who called the entire town one at a time and reminded them to vote for the special election. Baby brain was real.

"I'm the only one running." He started the engine. It was true, but it mattered to him that he had the support of the town, and I'd be damned if my vote wasn't among them. "Let's just get you to Doc's."

"Take me to vote." The words had more bite than I had meant them to. "Sorry."

"You're growing four babies. You can be grumpy if you want." He chuckled and drove me straight to town hall.

Good mate.

Town hall was lit up, a *Vote Here* sign on the front lawn. We didn't have forty locations—just the one, and it kind of amused me that they had the big sign.

"You got here just in time." Ms. Patty handed me a clipboard. "You need to sign in here and then I'll get you your ballot."

I signed and took the paper and headed back to the "booth" which turned out to be a school desk sitting behind a cubicle divider. On the way there, my stomach clenched and I froze, riding it out. I hated those stupid hicks things.

"You okay?" Ron asked.

"Yeah. Sorry. Be back in a second." I walked around the barrier and filled in my dot just as one of the babies rolled or kicked or whatever they did in there, and a warm wet sensation ran down my leg.

"Umm, Ms. Patty, can you come here?" I called out, not wanting to not get my vote turned in. "I have a question on this."

"Sure thing, honey." Two seconds later, she was by my side. "What do you need to know?"

"Here's my ballot and ummm, has Doc voted yet?"

"I can't tell you who...ohhhh...no. Not yet." Her eyes widened as they fell to the floor where there was currently a mess. How embarrassing!

"Did someone say my name?" Doc teased.

"Make him vote first," I whispered, and she nodded, scurrying off with my ballot.

"Here you go, Doc. You can just fill it out right here. Ron, just turn your head." That didn't sound fishy. Not at all.

Except by the sounds of things, they were just doing as she said.

"Thanks, Doc. I'll just run this through the ballot box."

"We were just coming to see you. Leo was thinking he wanted to double-check on the babies."

"I think you should go see him now," Ms. Patty spoke so calmly, but there must've been some gestures along with it because the next thing I knew, both Doc and Ron were flanking me and talking to each other about what they should be doing.

I didn't process one single word of it because a shooting pain ripped through me. It was similar to the Braxton Hicks contractions, but on crack, and for the first time since I discovered I was pregnant, I wasn't sure if I could do this.

"Honey, we're going to get you home." Ron's hand cupped my cheek. "Do you think you can do that?"

"Home...yes...home." I needed to be home. If I went to a hospital, all the human interventions would slow down my birth. The good thing about being a cat was that my delivery would come fast. Shit. It would come fast. I needed to get out of there. "Get me home."

Ron and Doc got me back to the van and home in record time, the contractions already at an evil level, and as much as I tried to bite back the pain to keep Ron from stressing and worrying more than he was, I couldn't.

"We'll get his clothes off and get him on the bed." Doc sounded far less worried than I felt.

Finally on the bed, all I wanted to do was to curl up in the fetal position, not that I could curl all the way. But I did my best, and it helped a lot. I'd never been present for a birth, but pride sex-ed class gave me some guidance about what to expect. Stupid internet only talked about human births. Doc just kept insisting it would become natural. There was nothing natural about being ripped in two.

"You'll probably want to push soon. Trust your body."

I trusted nothing.

Poor Ron looked helpless, something he hated being. "Should I boil water?"

"Only if you want tea." Doc chuckled. "How about you get the swaddle clothes I had you prepare ready. We're about to catch some babies." He wasn't wrong.

A half hour later, after pushing, cussing, and wondering if I was strong enough, our daughter Grace was born, followed by our son Travis, our son Aiden, and our daughter Francis.

"We have four babies." I sobbed, tears of joy flowing from my face as I held two babes to my chest and Ron held the other two by my side. "We did this."

"You did this, mate. You grew four perfect little—" He looked down at Doc. "What's wrong?"

Doc took the two babies from me and barked something about Ron putting the others in their bassinets.

"What's wrong?" Give me my babies back...except the last words didn't come out because I was...fading.

Something sharp pricked my arm. I couldn't flinch. I couldn't do anything but listen.

"Doc?" I'd never heard Ron sound so frightened.

"There's one more. I need to get them out before he bleeds out."

Ron kissed my forehead, his lips shaking. "You've got this, mate. You've. Got. This."

I wished he sounded more sure.

The pain—the pain was so much—different than before—sharper—like I was being cut open. I was being cut open...in my bed...in my home...awake but not. And just as I was about to fade into blackness, I heard a cry, a new cry, and everything was suddenly worth it.

"Wake up, love."

I tried to crack my eyes and gave up.

"Does he need you to help him shift again?" Ron asked. Shift again? I had no recollection of shifting, the last thing I remembered was...

"My babies." I forced my eyes open. "My babies."

"Are perfectly wonderful. All five of them." Doc squirted something into my mouth with a dropper. "Swallow that. You need to meet your babies."

"Come in, guys." Ron was sitting beside my bed, a baby in his arms. "This is Nessa."

"Like the monster?" I sat up and pushed myself against the headboard. How could he name our baby after a monster?

"Nessa means miracle. She is our smallest, and Doc says her heartbeat had been weak which was why we didn't notice her, but she came out fierce like a lion." He set her in my arms. "And don't worry, now that she's not being squashed by her siblings, she's perfect. And I already had a little discussion with her about how she's not allowed to almost kill her daddy again." He sang it like it was no big deal, but I had almost died...had I not been fighting for her I may have even welcomed it just to not be in the agony anymore.

"Knock, knock." Ms. Patty came in holding a baby, but I couldn't see which one from where I was. "We brought some people to visit you."

Jase, Edison, and Xander came in behind her, each carrying a baby, and August holding a sleeping Angeline.

"Papa said you should be dead." Xander set Grace in my other arm. "Said you fought harder than he's ever seen."

"Your papa is the one who saved her. I was just along for the ride."

Xander's face beamed with pride. I loved hearing him call Doc Papa. I hadn't known him when he was living here, in the awful conditions I'd walked into the day I moved in, but Doc was his father. Period.

"I appreciate the kind words, but don't underestimate your cat. He is fierce."

"Sheriff Ron." Ms. Patty handed him the baby in her arms, which turned out to be Travis. "Congratulations. Becoming a father of five beautiful children and the first person to get one hundred percent of the votes in the town elections. We didn't even get the yearly write-in for Scooby-Doo."

Small towns were weird.

I looked up at Ron with pride bursting out of my heart. "You won!"

"Oh, sweet mate of mine, I won the day I met you. You've given me a life I never dared to dream for, and now...five amazing children. If you could stop the almost dying thing, though, I'd appreciate that."

"I can do that." I looked around the room at my friends, my baby, and my mate.

Pride.

Once again, my cat was smarter than I was. These people...they were my pride. I was home.

Sometimes the past holds your future...

Omega otter shifter Doc loved his adopted son and wanted to protect him from his past. But when the boy's past flings itself at him in the form of a series of letters, Doc is faced with the heart wrenching decision of either ripping open old wounds or keeping unforgivable secrets from the child.

Rabbit shifter Levi hates his life as Alpha of his Colony. Put there by birthright and held there by his past, he has no choice: If he leaves, they will kill his one true mate. Rabbits were brutal like that.

When the colony is all abuzz with word of a stranger in town, Levi doesn't expect an otter and he certainly doesn't expect the man to be the bearer of both the worst and the best news of his life: His mate was gone and he had a son. And he most definitely doesn't expect to have his rabbit announcing the man as his mate.

Otterly Love is a sweet with knotty heat M/M shifter mpreg romance featuring an otter shifter looking out for his son, a rabbit shifter who fears he isn't strong enough to fix the wrongs of his path, an evil sheriff who won't stay gone, a boy who in some ways has more to teach his fathers then they have to teach him, true fated love, and an adorable little baby. This is the third book in the River's Edge Shifters series brought to you by the co-writing team of Lorelei M. Hart and Aria Grace and can be read as a stand alone. If you love knotty fun, true love, and your mpreg with heart, one-click today.

Order Now

Made in United States
North Haven, CT
17 February 2023

32786325R00129